"East Texas isn't like this, honey. Texas is a real place. Too real, sometimes," she said with a little sigh. "That's why this woman's got to leave it now and then if she wants to have a love life."

Frenchy stopped and a crowd of raucous teenagers carrying drinks swarmed around and passed them. "You mean I'm not the first woman you're meeting in Las Vegas?"

Gloria, about two inches taller, leaned to meet her eyes. Frenchy could see her cleavage where the cape parted, just above a gold-colored cocktail dress which shimmered in the blinking neon. "Honey," said Gloria, "practice makes perfect."

FOR

All the courageous women and men
who are standing up to the radical right.
Without them none of our stories could reach readers.

CACTUS LOVE

A collection of
short stories by

LEE LYNCH

THE NAIAD PRESS, INC.
1994

Printed in the United States of America on acid-free paper
First Edition

Edited by Christine Cassidy
Cover design by Bonnie Liss (Phoenix Graphics)
Typeset by Sandi Stancil

Library of Congress Cataloging-in-Publication Data

Lynch, Lee, 1945–
   Cactus love / by Lee Lynch
      p.   cm.
   ISBN 1-56280-071-X
   1. Lesbians—United States—Fiction.   I. Title.
PS3562.Y426C33   1994
813'.54—dc20
                                                        94-15979
                                                           CIP

CONTENTS

CREDITS

Thank you, Akia Woods, for your eager help and encouragement, your inspiring songs and strong spirit.

Thank you, Valerie Taylor and Hannah Blue Heron for your help with the Windy Sands stories. Thank you Selma Miriam and Susan Kenler for your assistance with "Hanukah At A Bar."

The following stories, some in slightly different form, originally appeared as noted:

"Truckstop Woman," *Lesbian Love Stories 2,* edited by Irene Zahava, The Crossing Press, 1991.
"The Wet Night," *Intricate Passions,* edited by Tee A. Corinne, Banned Books, 1989.
"The Big Bad Wolf," *Common Lives/Lesbian Lives,* Issue #27, Summer 1988.
"The Fires of Winter Solstice," *Just Out,* Volume 4, Number 3, January, 1987.
"Hanukkah At A Bar," *Common Lives/Lesbian Lives,* Issue #25, Winter 1988.
"Cactus Love," *Dykescapes,* edited by Tina Portillo, Alyson Publications, 1991 and *On Our Backs,* Volume 5, Number 4 March–April, 1989.
"Inez," *Pittsburgh's Out,* Issue #197, 8/93.

Lyrics from "Like A Mountain" used with permission of Naomi Littlebear Morena, Copyright Naomi Littlebear Morena, 1977.

TRUCK-STOP WOMAN
For Jodi Stutz, Writer
1958–1987

Jody'd been driving trailer trucks most of her life. Ever since she was a kid just starting out, she'd thought of herself as the Lone Ranger and called her trucks Silver. Her hot cab smelled of grease and rubber and the nutty home-cooked banana bread MayElla would send with her. When the hours got long on the macadam range, she'd recite old English ballads over the vibrations and shifting gears. Right now, at home, a favorite ballad rang through her head.

Thus in my sumptuous man's array
I bravely rode along the way . . .

The songs had always kept her company on the road and MayElla kept her company at home. She'd never minded the lonesomeness of trucking before.

She'd been tickled that the men on the road had never bothered her, despite a certain cavalier style she had and her striking violet eyes. For all her chattering and balladeering at home with MayElla, she had little to say in the rough independent world of the truckers. Besides, she'd been around forever, and when someone is around forever, even if she sticks out like a sore thumb, she becomes invisible. If the men were the only choice, she'd stay lonesome.

That's how she felt at the truck stops: invisible. She'd walk across a baking hot parking lot, ignoring the men, and enter the noisy restaurant. The cold of the air conditioning would feel like it could sear her skin. Once the waitresses figured out she was female, they frosted over too. She knew it was just because she scared them, in her GMC cap and her work clothes, but it hurt anyway. It shouldn't have mattered: she had no desire to talk to women who seemed to enjoy the ogling, the pinches, the bawdy jokes of the truckers. Over the years she'd gotten into the habit of leaving the turnpikes for meals even though it meant more distance and less pay. MayElla didn't mind. She said she would do the same thing.

MayElla had always been attractive to the men with her curvy top and her curvy sides, her spring-flower perfume and the way she'd put one

2

hand on a hip and kind of throw back her hair, then look you straight in the eye. Jody could hear her Nebraska twang even now, saying she'd had enough of being stared at and propositioned without going to some lowlife place it was bound to happen, like a truck stop.

So usually when Jody decided she couldn't keep her eyes open any longer, she'd head for the secondary roads and find a greasy spoon. Seldom the same one twice, though. And she never stayed in a motel. If someone with evil on his mind saw a truck by the side of the road, he was likely to believe there was another man inside. If he saw it was a lady driver registered for a room out in the middle of nowhere, with nobody around but a lot of screechy crickets, well, Jody didn't believe in asking for trouble. Let them go to the truck-stop girls who earned their living that way. They were even more lowlife than the waitresses.

She'd earned her living hauling freight for Standard Wheeling twenty-five years now and was proud of it. MayElla had cooked her a special dinner to celebrate that anniversary. It'd been just a week ago, that turkey dinner. Before they'd ever known MayElla had a heart problem. And now MayElla was dead and buried. Dead and buried, Jody repeated to herself, trying to make it real.

Jody'd never thought about this happening. They were only fifty-four, and they'd been together since they were kids when they'd lived across the hall from each other right here in Omaha. They'd just always liked being together. Both of their families had slipped down from their comfortable livings before the Depression to factory work. Neither their parents,

Jody nor MayElla had much use for the slummy little kids who were their neighbors, or for the games they played: King of the Mountain, which MayElla found too rough, or Hide and Seek, which Jody hated because she remembered being terrified that no one would ever find her. MayElla was always good at thinking up other games anyway.

Library was one. MayElla loved to be the librarian. There was a dark back hall which they agreed was lit just like the public library and smelled like it too, a little dusty, a little mildewy, a little mysterious. The stairs back there, which no one used, were the shelves. MayElla would set the books up. Jody contributed her stash of comics which MayElla called an Illustrated Encyclopedia. A few children's books lined the next shelf down, then came the *Reader's Digest* and *Good Housekeeping* magazines that people threw out. On the very bottom shelf were books belonging to MayElla's parents, a Bible and three volumes about World War I.

That was not all that was on the bottom shelf. Each year when MayElla won the poetry contest in school, her prize was a book. One year it had been Emily Dickinson, another Longfellow. Jody occasionally checked one of these out, mostly because MayElla was so proud of them.

The year MayElla won the book of old English ballads, though, Jody wouldn't return it. Those ballads caught her and pulled her in. She read them time after time and finally memorized some, just so she'd always have them with her. It felt like they matched her own inside rhythm and she'd found herself walking to school with their beat in her head.

O waly, waly, up the bank,
And waly, waly, doun the brae,
And waly, waly, yon burn-side,
Where I and my love wont to gae!

There were other games, games none of the
shouting, shoving children seemed to play. Like the
Roosevelts — Jody was Teddy, MayElla, Eleanor —
who traveled the world together, leaving the boring
task of government to Franklin D. It was as if in
childhood the two of them had been marked to
prepare differently for the different life they would
live. Given dreams they would not share with anyone
but each other. They were careful, even then, not to
reveal their world to anyone who would sully it.

MayElla had prepared well for the life she wanted.
She went to library school, supporting herself as a
gal Friday. Though she'd hated working with the
common girls at Standard Wheeling, the trucking
company she'd worked for just before graduation,
she'd made the most of it.

None of the choices schooling had offered seemed
to suit Jody. She'd taken a job after high school
delivering messages on a three-wheeled motorbike, but
wished she could see some of the country. MayElla
bragged to her boss at Standard Wheeling about
Jody's perfect driving record and convinced him to
take a chance on her. She'd been on the road ever
since.

One of those little grey birds that MayElla always
fed was on the window sill, up like her at the crack
of dawn. Jody rose, a stiffness in her back from the
years of driving. The whole loaf in the bread box was
stale, so she broke all of it up for the birds. What in

heck would they do with her away on the road and
no MayElla to overfeed them? Never mind the birds,
what in heck was she going to do without the games,
without the poems. How could those birds sing now?
How could she?

> And then my love built me a bower,
>   Bedeck'd with many a fragrant flower;
> A braver bower you ne'er did see
>   Than my true love did build for me.

Well, she had a load to pick up. She locked the
door and for the first time in a week went out to the
tractor, zipping up her company jacket. She pulled
herself into the seat of the cab, glad for something to
do. Glad Silver hadn't changed.

But he had. He still smelled of rubber and grease,
but the fresh-baked banana bread? For a minute she
couldn't see through the mist of tears across her
eyes. Everything really was the same, except for what
MayElla had touched. And MayElla had touched
everything.

She started the truck without even thinking. Its
vibrations, its low roar, were comforting. They
reminded her that she was a driver. That hadn't
changed. She heaved a sigh. She hadn't cried yet and
she wasn't about to cry now. In the first place, it
was hard to drive when your eyes were burning with
salty tears. In the second place, what if somebody
along the way saw her, a truck driver, crying. Third,
if she let loose just once, she felt like everything
would change. Like MayElla being away was just part
of how different things would be. She was afraid she
might just let Silver run off the road, aimed for a

bank of trees or a concrete wall or a cliff. Just *anything* so she could be with MayElla again.

She squared her shoulders, put the truck in gear and went over to Standard Wheeling. She hitched up her trailer, full of something, it didn't matter what, just so she could buy bread for MayElla's birds. Sooner or later she had to start eating again too. They gave her papers and she saw she was going to Oklahoma with pallets of dog food. Dog food, of all things, to keep her going through life. Well, it paid the bills.

She hit the highway, window rolled up to keep out the early morning chill. The miles of Interstate 29, then 35, felt as familiar as home. Sometimes she thought half the reason she took to the road was to get home again. To crawl under the covers and listen to MayElla in the dark, or to recite ballads till MayElla, still excited that Jody had come to love words too, reached for her and quieted her with warm lips that told poems silently to Jody's mouth.

O waly, waly, gin love be bonie
A little time while it is new!

Jody passed through the suburbs of Omaha, trying not to think about home. They'd liked the city all right, but then they'd bought the Ford. MayElla always had a yen for greenery, so when the garden apartments were built on some old farm-land just out of town, they'd rented a one bedroom brand new and had been there eighteen years.

MayElla loved to plant flowers outside their place on a spring weekend. She'd get Jody to go out and turn the soil before the baseball games started on

TV. The baseball games that MayElla *always* hated. But it worked out fine, especially in the summers. MayElla, letting the back screen door make that summer *thwomp* sound behind her, would take her books to read in the scent of new-mowed lawn. She'd admire the flowers she'd put in, pass the time of day with the neighbors, stare out at the horizon, and make up poems in her head.

It was the same with the neighbors as it was at the truck stops. They just didn't seem to see Jody. Oh, the men might tip their hats, eyes to the ground, the women nod with automatic smiles, but no one stopped to talk as they did with MayElla. It was as if, like the waitresses, they didn't want to see her. It didn't matter when the waitresses acted snippy and walked away, but she knew it hurt MayElla that the neighbors worked at pretending she wasn't there, *that one living with pretty Miss Bowen.*

She passed out of Nebraska and into Kansas. The steering wheel felt warm and comfortingly solid in her hands, the sound of the shifting gears like friends greeting her. The sun kept getting brighter, but it was fall and strong. She was glad it wasn't spring yet, when MayElla's perennials would come up like poems in color.

It wasn't that everything had gone smoothly all the time. They'd had their spats. One or the other might grump around the house for hours, sure she was right. Now and then they'd face away from each other in bed at night, unable to untangle some mess they'd talked themselves into. It didn't take a whole lot to get unsnarled, though. Jody would bring home a batch of flowers. MayElla would apologize by lying beside her in the dark, telling a new poem. It always melted Jody's heart.

What was she going to do now? Who would hold her, listen to her, help her get through this? They'd never wanted, needed anyone but each other. Their families thought that they were just friends. It would make it easier if she could show how bad she felt, but show her straight-laced mother, her deacon father?

> *O mother, mother, make my bed,*
> *O make it soft and narrow;*
> *Since my love died for me today,*
> *I'll die for him tomorrow.*

The rhythm soothed her almost all the way to Oklahoma City.

The dispatcher had given her a choice: either turn around in Oklahoma or go all the way out to California. There were loads either way. "It's warm in California," the dispatcher had said. Jody could tell none of the other drivers had wanted to go all the way to the west coast. She joked with him, letting him know she knew what he was up to, making him think she was doing him a favor. She knew even before he asked that she didn't want to come back to Nebraska for a while. Couldn't. Not till she'd gotten past this inside churning she was going through, not till she had a way of not hurting so badly all the time.

Another old time driver nodded hello to her at the depot in Oklahoma City. He was headed home. Home to a wife probably. Not many people lost a mate this young.

9

It was just as if she and MayElla had been married all those years. Married people had their wakes and sympathy and the head car in the procession. Jody'd had — well she'd been seated in the second row at the church, but MayElla's family acted as if she was supposed to give them consolation, not the other way around. She'd waited till the funeral was over before she'd gone to the cemetery.

Then she'd just stared through the rain down at the coffin into that damned hole in the earth, not feeling at all connected to what was inside of it. She'd stared and waited for something to happen. All that had happened was the machine had come to cover the coffin over and she'd walked carefully away on the muddy grass, in her family occasion dress-up shoes, back to the Ford, Ford number three.

Ever since, she'd felt all twisted up inside and couldn't get unknotted, like she used to feel during a fight. No one was claiming to be right or wrong this time, though. No one was coming to bed that night with a poem to make it better. And all the flowers she'd made sure were at the funeral wouldn't make a bit of difference sitting up on top of a mound of earth. She would at least have liked to turn over the soil, like she'd done so many times for MayElla's plants.

> *And then my love built me a bower*
> *Bedeck'd with many a fragrant flower . . .*

She started driving out of Oklahoma with dark coming on, grateful the company had been anxious to get this new load to California because she was full again in no time. She drove straight through to the middle of the night, to Texas, before her eyes wanted to close. She'd been hallucinating figures out on the road for an hour.

She didn't want to leave the straight line of the highway when everything else in her life felt so strange. At an enormous truck stop she pulled in next to a line of rigs. There was a motel, a restaurant, a truck store, showers, a Laundromat. The neon signs, the red and gold lights outlining some of the idling trucks, the fluorescent bars of light flooding the pump area, gave the flat cement world a partying look, like a carnival was setting up right in the middle of the Panhandle.

Here and there she saw a truck-stop girl accost a driver. Why didn't these women do something clean and useful, like drive a truck or work in a library? Sometimes the momentary couple would disappear into a room, sometimes into a truck.

The quick and the dead, Jody thought, remembering the phrase from some poem MayElla had recited. She'd always wondered what life was like for these truck-stop girls. At least they were quick, not dead, she thought with a bitter anger.

She stretched and yawned, but that small pleasure only unleashed her pain. She leaned her head against the hard narrow steering wheel. How could she feel good when there MayElla was, in that box, as if she were playing one last game. She hit the steering wheel with a fist. MayElla had promised never to leave her out!

Jody swung open the door of the truck and stepped down with a groan, her back aching from the drive, her anger tying the knot inside even tighter. She gulped the cold night air, relishing the familiar smells of fuel and oil and a lone cigarette somewhere on the lot. Though food seemed like a waste, she knew she'd never make the rest of the trip without it and she strode toward the restaurant.

"Nice evening, mister," she heard a voice coo from the shadow of another truck. A lady's voice.

She scowled toward the voice and said, "Howdy," as gruffly as she could. It was one of the truck-stop girls.

"Whoops," said the girl. "I thought you were a guy!"

It had happened before.

"Sorry!" the girl called to her back.

Jody crunched along the gravel toward the restaurant. She wondered what it was like for the men, these anonymous contacts in flat parking lots. Was it just for the sex? It was disgusting, she'd always thought, but maybe some of them were widowers, or had never had someone to come home to. Maybe sometimes they just wanted to be held.

The girls, though, why did they do this? She pictured the slummy little neighbor kids of forty-five years ago, the ones she and MayElla had refused to play with. Did some of those little girls later lurk alongside trucks or in Omaha doorways, selling themselves? For the first time Jody felt a kind of link with those little girls. They were in their fifties now too. What had happened to them? Were their lives over like hers? What did it matter in the end if you wrote poetry or whispered *Hey, mister* at strangers?

Inside the restaurant there were enough diners to keep two waitresses busy. The air conditioning was on too high. The cigarette smoke smelled stale. She moved a dirty ashtray aside and stared at the jukebox on the counter, feeling as if she hadn't seen one in years. She used to play a song or two while she ate, just to hear the poetry, or to take a rhythm with her on the road. Dinner was her usual mashed potatoes, stringy pot roast, peas and carrots with a wilted salad in a small heavy side dish. The dinner roll was cold, but the coffee was scalding hot and helped her wash it all down. Only one thing was different. The waitress was friendly.

"Where you from, sister?" asked the sharp-faced woman with a weary warm smile.

Jody was afraid that she would break down right then.

"Long ways from home, aren't you?" commented the waitress a while later, warming her coffee. She looked, under the cosmetics, to be about Jody's age.

Jody tried to mumble an answer to this too, but all that wanted to come out was, "I love you," and at her silence the waitress shrugged and turned away. Now why would she want to say that to the waitress, to anybody, with MayElla dead? Her eyes filled with tears. When she stood she felt dizzy. Maybe she was the one who was different.

"You okay, kiddo?" asked that same waitress.

What must she look like to the woman: stooped, grayhaired, staggering like a drunk. "Just tired," answered Jody, straightening. She didn't need the concern of some all-night waitress with makeup plastered on her face.

The chilled fresh air was so clear it seemed to kiss her awake. The wide open spaces of the Panhandle touched her right in her soul. She felt small and mean for thinking poorly of the waitress. On the highway trucks roared by, restless, pushing west or east. She stood off to the side of the restaurant watching the stars blink. Could MayElla be something like a star now, up there, looking down and loving her, wishing her well?

How *could* she be well, Jody asked the stars, feeling a new flash of anger. Could she play games by herself? How about, Pretend Someone's Home, Waiting. There was nothing back there. MayElla's family had taken everything away with them, even the poetry books MayElla had so carefully written out by hand. That poetry wasn't for them. It wouldn't keep them alive. "Tell me what to do now!" she whispered faintly through her trapped tears, to the prettiest star.

> *Marti'mas wind, when wilt thou blaw,*
> *And shake the green leaves aff the tree?*
> *O gentle death, when wilt thou come?*
> *For of my life I am wearie.*

The anger drove her back toward her rig. Maybe dinner hadn't been a good idea. Maybe she ought to drive on now, and let Silver take her over a cliff.

"Hey, mister — oh, it's you again."

Jody stopped and looked at the woman this time. She was on the tall side, sturdily built in tight fashion jeans, ruffled Western blouse and wine-colored short vinyl jacket. Even in the shadow of the trucks the woman, who might be part American Indian, looked tired and had lines on her face, as if she had her troubles too.

"What're you looking at? Didn't you ever see a lady of the night before?"

Jody felt herself flush. "I'm just —" How could she

say it, what she felt inside? The air out here, the way she'd felt touched by something as big as, bigger than these western spaces. She began to tremble. Here was a woman, flesh and blood just like her. For rent, maybe, but warm and alive. She shivered, pulled her Standard Wheeling jacket closed and zipped it up. That pretty star caught her eye.

What if she did play a game tonight. Just this once. What if she pretended that star was MayElla, and this woman the friend MayElla thought she ought to have to listen to her, to give her the sympathy MayElla's folks, the neighbors, no one else had given her. Maybe even to hold her. No!

When cockle-shells turn silver bells,
And mussells grow on every tree,
When frost and snow turns fire to burn,
Then I'll sit down and dine wi' thee.

Well, maybe them cockle shells were turning to silver bells, thought Jody, taking a deep breath. And maybe it was about time.

"Listen," she said to the woman. Awkwardly she grabbed her trucker's wallet on the chain she wore clipped to a belt loop. With a bill in her shaking hand she said, "My name is Jody. My lady just passed on. Can you —" she offered the bill, seeing the woman all wavery through the tears that would not wait another minute — "can you spend a little time with me? Just to —" The woman looked startled. Jody thought she was going to back off. Could she get the truck out of here in time to outrun the cops? To outrun her humiliation?

But the woman was saying, "You poor thing. Haven't you got anybody else in the whole world?"

Jody's ears roared with tears which sounded like the trucks going by. "No," she admitted, hoarsely.

The woman took the money. "Come on with me, Jody. I have a little room over in the motel. I want you to come tell me all about it. My name's Michelle."

Michelle's words were as simple as a ballad. Her eyes, when a truck rolled in across from them, shone like a star's. As she felt the tears fall, Jody thought there might even be a little bit of MayElla in those eyes. MayElla in a truck-stop woman. Who would have guessed?

The dry Panhandle wind sang across the parking lot like an old English rhythm. She followed Michelle.

WINDY AND VAN

At five foot two, I'll swear I'm taller by a full inch since I retired early in 1968. The best move I ever made, though the Motor Vehicle Department wanted me to stay. I was good at my job, kept the drivers laughing, got them out fast. Maybe I'm just standing straighter, knowing they wanted me and I got away, knowing I'm free as a roadrunner.

When I look in the mirror I see an Old Woman cactus. Just like the white-haired torch cactus most folks call Old Man, I can pass for a gnomish grandfather. Too many years out here on the desert all by myself. The gang at Motor Vehicles ought to see me now in my big old straw hat that's ready for the trash heap, lording it over my empire of rusty trailers, shacks and shanties — and the hothouses that make up my business, the Windy Sands Cactus Ranch.

You've heard it on Tucson radio: *"Stick with us — we'll grow on you!"* That's me. The retail end of this business is more trouble than a fishtail cactus that's got it in for you. Most of the small businessmen around here have their wives to help them. My life would be simpler if I had a wife too. But I've learned my lesson in love: it's not worth it. So I've been trying for an age to get someone decent to manage the darned shop.

"What I want from you, honey," I told the next to last applicant I interviewed, who wore a teensy gold cross around her neck, "is the gumption to run this operation like your life depended on it, meaning working twelve hours a day like I do, getting in there and dirtying your fingernails, taking orders from me whether you agree with them or not, and never, never bothering me with details unless I ask for them."

I gave her my best coyote squint, saw her look at how the desert sun had turned my complexion red-brown and wrinkly. Then I leaned forward on my favorite old wooden swivel chair, fists on my knees to show her I meant business. "Do you think you can handle it?"

Her eyes looked terrified. "Oh, yes," she answered sweet as pie.

"Bullshit!" I barked. She jumped like a startled

18

toad. "You haven't got the backbone of a gecko. You might do for a flower stand, but not for a cactus ranch. Do us both a favor: go on back to town and get yourself a civilized job."

The woman got up like I'd just said her chair was on fire. She smoothed her skirt over her legs, seemed like she was going to answer, but changed her mind and skedaddled. I heard her starter grind three times before the she managed to get on the road. I kind of wished I had someone to laugh with about it.

But I don't. Never was able to hold a woman long. Don't know why I keep wishing. The dogs, two small poodles I'd taken in when an old friend of mine died, came and sat to either side of me, panting, looking like they adored me. I don't treat them like powder puffs, either. They're smart, good company and devoted. That's all I ask.

I swiveled my chair around and rode it to my desk like a burro. There was one application left.

I gave my old DMV cheer, just like a line of drivers were grumbling out in the hothouse. "Van Bourne!"

She was quick. I liked that. She came striding through my office door with big round horned-rim glasses perched over a tiny sharp nose, and brows arched over them. Her face was all huge startled eyes, like an elf-owl under a flashlight.

"Did I surprise you?"

"No, ma'am," answered Van Bourne, standing over me, wearing her thirty-odd years with authority. I wondered what her Achilles heel would turn out to be.

"Sit down, girl. Don't stand on ceremony with me."

That wide-eyed look stayed, but she was grinning ear to ear, like the one look at me told her all she needed to know.

I rattled the girl's application for a while. You can't just hire someone on sight.

"You ever steal from an employer?"

"No."

"Hide your mistakes?"

"No."

"Quit without notice?"

"No."

"Slack off on your job?"

"When I was a kid. At Pizza Hut."

"I would've too. Do you learn quick?"

"Yes."

"How'd you end up a prison guard?" I jabbed, thinking this was good experience to keep the customers honest.

"I needed a job and thought I could do it better than some people, with my college training."

"Did you?"

"I hope so."

"Why'd you leave?"

"I kept feeling it could be me in there, if I hadn't had a few breaks in my life. Didn't feel like I had a right to be outside when those women were in."

"And the nursery you managed?"

"I thought I'd feel more comfortable telling plants what to do. Some of my friends worked there. We had a good time. The boss couldn't believe a bunch like us could bring his sales up so high and keep his store looking so good."

"A bunch like you?"

Without hesitation, Van answered, "Gays." She watched me through those big calm elf-eyes.

I couldn't help smiling. I leaned forward and offered my hand, callouses and all. "Glad to meet you. What brings you to Tucson?"

Van shook hands like she walked, quick, purposeful, without taking her eyes off mine.

"My grandmother. She raised me. I followed her down just in case she needs me. She lives in that senior housing complex out by the air base."

"Bet she enjoys those bombers doing their trial runs all day."

"Says they make her feel secure." Van shrugged. "We don't agree on much, but she's all the family I've got."

"Seems to me she's got a point about security."

Van just smiled.

"Tell me what you'd do to improve this place." I wanted to know what the ranch looked like to those young eyes.

Van looked around the office, as if she could see all of the operation from her seat.

"The whole thing takes up about four desert acres," I told her, hoping I was training her as I did. "Half an acre in young trees. The rest hothouses, full of tables covered with cactus plants and succulents. The walls are half corrugated metal, half clear plastic, except where these old wooden buildings are standing. It started as a weekend hobby, but it grew like purplemat in early spring. I told the people at work what I was doing and they flocked out here like tourists. Who'd have thought there'd be such a thirst for cactus in the desert?"

Van had an earnest look on her face. "I don't

21

know enough about the business to suggest improvements yet. Maybe there don't need to be improvements. I'd want to take things a little slower than that."

"I need you to start right now, today. I open in an hour and I fired the last manager two days ago. I'm backed up on my other work."

"No problem."

"Where do you live?"

"I'm in a fleabag motel off Stone."

"If you're interested, I have an old trailer I can let you have for the upkeep. I wouldn't mind someone else on the property. Might keep an edge off the lonesomes on a Saturday night."

She gave me a sharp look, like she was wary that I was wanting an ear to bend on my time off. Well, maybe I was.

"I'd like to take a look at the trailer. After work," she answered slowly. I just about kept myself from doing a jig.

This time, it was Van who offered her hand. I watched for the warm smile again, but the elf only nodded solemnly, like she feared to jinx her good luck. I wondered what made her so scared when I was sure she'd be a success.

That was in March. We had a lot of rain for that time of year, washing away what seemed like half the outskirts of Tucson. The usual reckless teenager had got swept into a washout in his pickup, the papers screamed about flooding, then the land dried up quicker than a jackrabbit dodging tourist cars and May came, the month when the saguaros, the whole desert, and the last of the vacation invasion bloomed.

There's nothing better than the return of that clean-smelling dry air.

I was bushed from supplying Van with plants. She sold them faster than my nursery crew could get them in pots. Pincushions, necklace vines, angel wings, ruby balls, and painted ladies: I saw them in my dreams. Maybe she noticed how tired I was, maybe she was just proud of her little trailer. It was right after the Memorial Day weekend that she invited me to dinner for the first time.

The trailer showed the same care as her shop did. The inside and outside had been scrubbed, patched and stripped of the old fixtures. The interior was one big room now. A few comfortable pieces of secondhand furniture made it homey, but not crowded. She'd built a slender sleeping loft over a space that held a TV and stereo, books and a chest of drawers.

All around and over the trailer she'd put up a ramada. I sat under the thin slats of light and shade, feet up on a milk crate, and swilled some kind of red-colored iced tea that tasted like water. Van worked in the camp kitchen she'd built by setting a stove and refrigerator outside the trailer. I could remember being as energetic when Dad died, leaving me the four acres and his sagging shack.

"My empire," I said as Van served the beans and rice. "This whole place began as nothing more than a falling down wooden building."

"Then what happened?" asked Van. She wore a modified cowboy hat with a flashy red band around the crown.

"Then I bought this trailer. Then a bigger trailer.

When I needed a building for the cactuses, I put in plumbing, had the electric run out here, got my trailer just right. I do prefer a trailer house. I like the feeling I can get up and go any old time."

"But you've always lived in Tucson."

"I like to think I could leave it all behind. I will someday."

Van looked up.

"Everybody has to kick the bucket sooner or later, though I'm not sure I believed that at your age. I won't be fussing about living in Tucson then."

We were quiet for a while, eating. A car whooshed by over on Mile Wide Road. The cactus wrens, shouting *chug, chug, chug, chug, chug,* sounded like they were having their Saturday evening bash. A warbler flicked its tail feathers at us, rummaging like an early bird at a garage sale. The land smelled hot, and spicy from dinner.

Van dabbed at the sheen of sweat under her glasses. She looked so innocent with those big round eyes. And she held her head just like the little elf owls, tilted to one side. She'd brought her grandma out a couple of times, and darned if the lady didn't look just like her, only smaller and wiser.

Tonight, though, as the sun started to dip like a yellow bucket after water, I noticed something new about those eyes. In the shop Van was always busy; I zoomed around too fast to see anything but dirt and pots and moisture levels. There were shadows under her eyes as dark as noontime shade.

"Did you ever think of another kind of life?" Van asked, like she knew where my thoughts were.

"I *had* another life," I told her. "Lived in town,

worked for the state, went to the club every Saturday night."

"Alone, though?" she asked. "Always alone?"

Those eyes were aging by the second.

"I suppose Cupid could've been kinder to me," I admitted, setting down my fork. I leaned back in the easy chair that Van had pushed me into. "No," I decided on reflection, "Cupid didn't do a darned thing wrong. There were plenty of willing women." The warbler chitted some, like she was encouraging me to bare my soul. I looked back out to the desert. This wasn't the youngster's business, not a bit of it, but I could still see those hungry eyes in front of me. Where had I gone for answers at her age? "I just couldn't hang onto a one of them, that's all."

Van stopped eating altogether then. When I glanced her way she was all eyes and ears.

"I always thought I was a giver," I explained. "I'd buy them things, move them in with me, cook, clean, do the lovemaking — all of it. After a while I'd get sick of it and start to stew. Then, next thing I knew, I'd be fooling around with someone new, head over heels in love." The first cool breeze of evening drifted by, in no hurry, and rattled the leaves of a real old paloverde that shaded the outhouse. "If I had as many friends in this town as ex-lovers, I'd never be lonesome."

Van looked like she didn't believe my burst of laughter. She was right. The day had been long, my face was gritty from dust, my eyes stung from sunlight. I'd skipped my usual nap, ironing my yellow Western shirt to wear to dinner. I felt flat and empty admitting my failure at love. "So I married me a cactus ranch. The little varmints may be prickly as women, but they don't make me stew."

Van took off her hat and swept back her sweaty hair. She fanned herself with the hat. "They blossom for you," she said.

I was tickled that she'd noticed.

We were quiet a while, picking at the last of dinner, listening to the birds. Then Van asked, "Are there turtles out here?"

"They're called desert tortoises."

"That's what I feel like. Pulling my house over my back and settling in."

"You left some lady behind too?"

"She was paroled last month," Van said in a small voice.

So here's the chink in your armor, I thought. I knew the story without another word. She told it anyway.

"I never touched her. She was a prisoner, I was a guard. I would've lost my job, she would've lost her chance at parole. It was the looking that did it, those hot looks, and a word here and there that left me out of breath. I slipped her my address before I left and dreamed of her every night since then. But I've heard that jailhouse love is like growing cacti," Van said with a sigh. "Your success rate goes down with transplanting. She wants to come here."

"And you?"

"I'm not sure I want anyone under my shell with me, especially not with her history."

I didn't want to know about it. I'd found love hard enough with the simplest and most commonplace of women. "It sounds to me as if you are headed in exactly the right direction, partner," I told Van. "Out."

She looked around my spread. "Don't you ever wish you had someone to share all this with?"

My answer was quicker than a roadrunner crossing the Speedway. "No. I'm through with love."

It was another month before Ivy showed up. I saw the attraction right away, when Van introduced us. Ivy was pretty, in her early twenties, with thick strawberry-blonde hair, maybe not her true color, and a real feminine way about her. I couldn't imagine what she'd been locked up for, and never did ask. There was just the one meeting, and then a glimpse of her now and then in the early morning, after she'd stayed with Van.

I imagined what went on in that little old trailer of mine, but Van had installed an air conditioner, so I couldn't hear a thing. All I knew was that Van didn't stop smiling from dawn to dusk for the length of the summer. She seemed to smile biggest when that Ivy waltzed around in her skimpy bare-shouldered tops and the short shorts that made my underpants look like coveralls. After jail uniforms, I decided, the woman needed some freedom. I wondered, though, just how much freedom she was taking while poor Van sweated in the hothouse shop, and with whom.

"I don't own her," Van insisted one time when I made a remark about the unreliable nature of women in general.

"You mean you wouldn't mind if she went with someone else too?"

"Mind? Yes, I'd mind. But what could I do? Half of me is still scared she's even here, and is glad for her independence." Her glasses glinted in the sun when she laughed. "The other half wants to tie her down and marry her."

Van took a customer then, and I went back to my office, where I fought with columns of numbers till I couldn't see straight. Why was I having such a problem with the books today?

A few days later, at closing time, I heard my nursery workers slam their car doors, the usual tires on sandy gravel. Then unexpected footsteps crossed to my office. I wondered if Van had come back early from the Tanque Verde Greenhouses, where I'd sent her to work a trade on the items we can't seem to move and they can't keep on the tables.

But Van wouldn't knock at the door like this. I was on the phone with a supplier and yelled for the knocker to come on in. It was Ivy. She looked like a thunderstorm and stood tapping her foot, letting every flying insect in Southern Arizona inside while she propped the screen door open. I finished my business pretty quick.

"Y'all know where Van got herself to?"

The woman's hair was frazzled, her eyes wild, but she stood perfectly still now, as if her life depended on my answer.

I turned on my burro chair to check the calendar. "Let's see," I said, purposely slow and dumb, just by instinct. "It's a Tuesday, isn't it?"

"Yes," came the answer through her teeth, like a snake impatient to make its strike.

"Then she's over on the other side of town at the greenhouses."

She was out the door before I'd finished and I was immediately sorry I'd spilled the beans. Damn! What if this youngster went over to Tanque Verde and raised some kind of ruckus? That was when I thought to look at the time. Six o'clock! Van would be long gone from there, probably stopped somewhere on the Speedway for groceries.

The tiny pang of guilt I felt for telling Ivy wrong propelled me from my chair. The car was just pulling out as I yelled. No one heard me. It was a convertible, sporty and yellow. The driver looked like a long-haired pimp. They drove hell-bent for leather toward Mile Wide Road, raising more grit than a dust devil. What kind of people had Ivy taken up with in town?

Though I searched Van's eyes the next day, I read nothing except business there. The yellow car did not return. Saturday night, as usual, Van went to town and brought Ivy back with her, late.

This was none of my business, and I didn't think too much about it. I was gladder than a rancher with his first bob-wire fence that whatever dramas were stampeding through Van's life, I was long past them. Still, I missed Van's cheek-busting smile from the first month that Ivy was in town, those eyes that looked like they'd just seen paradise, the loosened walk of a well-loved woman. I knew something wasn't right. I asked her to dinner at my place this time.

I barbecued up some beef for us, with nice hot refried beans. I was bound not to pry.

"How's your love life?" my windy old mouth asked before I could stop it.

"Gee," she answers, the elf owl in the flesh — or feathers.

29

Then she takes a huge bite of the beans and lets out a howl. By the time I'd poured six gallons of water down her throat she'd had the chance to get us on a new subject and didn't stop talking all night. I'd never known Van to be shifty before. I started to worry for real.

Ivy didn't come home with her the next weekend, nor the next. I didn't have a minute to observe Van, though, because one of my exes, who'd been through cancer more times than I'd thought a body could stand it, was in her final illness. I was spending every other night with her, and all of the weekend days, to spell her lover. In my time off I was trying to keep up with the ranch and my life, but it wasn't possible, not at my age. I left a lot of the business in Van's hands those three weeks, and she did such a fine job I stayed on when my ex passed away to help make the arrangements and go through her affairs.

I came back with my truck Pickup Nellie piled high, full of a bunch of junk her lover and me didn't want. I thought Van might like some of the furniture and Arizona knickknacks.

I hadn't asked if I could drop by to talk about the booty. But I was feeling so low that I meandered over after supper with the dogs. Spending all that time with my ex had brought back a flood of memories, not every one of them bad. She was a fine-looking woman, even at the end. We'd danced till midnight and beyond many a Saturday when there was no TV, no money for anything else. Just whirling around and around a barroom floor, glad to have a place out of sight of the kind of folks who'd do us in first chance they'd get, grateful if the bar wasn't raided that weekend. Emma was her name. Emma, my golden girl, I'd called her.

There was shouting coming from the little trailer. I stopped at the corner of the last hothouse.

I recognized Emma's voice. Emma? Couldn't be. It was Ivy. I heard something crash against a window. I felt the old horror that love could turn to such rage.

"OUT!" bellowed Van. I peered around the side of the hothouse and saw that she was trying to push Ivy through the door. "I told you I didn't want you like this!"

Ivy staggered out, her laugh like an angry jay's screech. "You're so straight you might as well still be wearing your uniform, screw!" Ivy taunted.

"I won't even give you the courtesy of a ride home if you can't shut your mouth, Ivy!" Van yelled as she pulled the door shut behind her.

I watched her hustle the woman into her little pickup and run around to her side. The whole scene had taken less than three minutes and they were gone.

My stomach churned. How many times had I lived through just such a short, fiery hell? Even with Emma.

I heard her brakes squeal at the stop sign up the road. The dust was settling outside her trailer. The land was serene again, the warblers and wrens beginning to sing their twilight songs. I wondered if this really would be the end of Ivy for Van, if she would pull her house over her back and stay inside, like I'd done when I wasn't much older than her.

Look at the damage love brought to perfectly happy women! Loneliness wasn't much of a price to pay for peace, was it?

I headed back to my trailer with the dogs. A coyote yipped off toward the hills. I loved this place, I loved my life, I hated the fuss and bother of women, but I couldn't get Van's cheek-busting smile out of my mind. When was the last time I'd smiled like that?

Harvest time came on this year all of a sudden, swooping down like the Great Revenuer from the sky. The asters, the fleabane, are dying out. Great bunches of yellow desert broom are the only things around to please the eye.

It only took till now, November, for me and Van to settle into our routine: I make supper for her every Saturday night that she isn't making supper for me. Sometimes she'll go into town afterwards.

Sometimes now, I go with her.

I'm not looking for somebody. Van and Ivy's last fight makes me think twice before I ask anyone to dance.

On the other hand, it's one thing to be pleased that you raised a beautiful cactus, a whole other thing for a smile to take up residence on your face. Even for a little while.

Ivy ended up in prison again. She got picked up shoplifting makeup and sent back to Arkansas for breaking parole — she wasn't supposed to be in Arizona. So I suppose you could say she's gone to jail for love, for wanting to be with Van.

Who is looking again.

Sometimes I think we just keep repeating our crimes over and over. Some of us do get put in prison. Some of us lock ourselves up for self-protection.

Windy Sands is coming up for parole again. I'm on my best behavior.

CANNON STREET

Cannon Street was as ordinary as daylight. Still, when she rounded that last corner of worn red brick sidewalk laid probably a hundred years ago, she always caught her breath. The street only cut through a neighborhood, but it was her avenue of spectacle and adventure.

There was a tree outside the beige apartment building on the other corner, and on that day the tree dangled russet leaves. From beneath the tree she could look far along the street and see women pulling shopping carts behind them, purses dangling from their arms, could see high school kids like herself explosive on their holiday, and men bumping and rattling empty dollies over curbs. She could see from under those last leaves the length of Cannon Street lined with parked, double-parked and honking vehicles, past the two-block shopping district with its guardian candy stores, one at each end, past the pharmacy with its lunch counter, past the new grocery store, the cleaners, the dark, coffee-scented A&P, the hushed card shop that rented cellophane-wrapped hardcover books, past the French bakery with lacy chocolate-topped cookies, pastel *petit fours* and that sweet hot bread smell, past the hardware store with its bins of mysterious gadgets, its wooden floor so used each plank was cupped and sound seemed muffled by the old walls, past the bicycle shop packed to the rafters with blue fat-wheeled cruisers and shiny green three-speeds and red wagons, red sleds, red scooters with a dozen different raucous black-bulbed horns and shiny handlebar bells in the window, and upstairs along the street the signs of accountants and dentists, the old coin dealer, the costume and tuxedo rental shop — she could see from under the old beech tree how the street stretched out of sight to the fusty old cannon perched at its far end, forever poised for one more salute.

There were also a barber shop and two hairdressing salons on Cannon Street. When she was a little kid the barber had sufficed, and she would run her fingers around the swirling, glass-smooth red, white and blue-striped pole on her way in, but a year and a half ago when she'd become a teenager, her mother had switched her over to the Elegante Beauty

Shoppe. Mr. Jack, who had the hairy arms and balding head of a barber, owned the Shoppe with his wife. He had prettied up Ericka's dutchboy cut, feathered it and shingled it and given her itty bitty pointy sideburns as if he could make a pixie of her. Each time she walked out of the nauseating odors into the fresh air she felt like someone had switched ballet slippers for her white sneaks and bobby socks. Each time she lost her footing and had to find her own walk all over again.

Today her mother had given her the money and told her to say hello to Mr. Jack. Hands in her pockets, whistling jaunty tunes for courage, she hugged the buildings across the street from the Elegante and counted cracks in the slate sidewalk, avoiding the eyes of every shopper that passed, hoping it was too chilly for Mr. Jack to be lounging outdoors with a cigarette. There was a dazzling new display of baseball cards in the window of her favorite candy store and the donut delivery man happened past with a trayful that smelled like the cinnamon crullers Grandpa dunked in his milky coffee. Afterward, she'd come back.

Before she knew it she was past Snip'N'Shape, the other beauty salon. She panicked, stopped, felt conspicuous, went on. She could turn around and go in, but they might have noticed that she'd missed the shop on her first try. As it was, a woman she recognized as the mother of a ninth grade classmate smiled at her. She tripped on a deep sidewalk crack, fled into the deli and pretended to look around. This palace of German sausage and tins of foreign crackers, of loud orders in a foreign tongue, of hanging bolognas and hard salamis sliced paper-thin, of sawdust and a wooden pickle barrel — she had fifty cents of her own. She uncovered the barrel, took the cold steel tongs from the side and fished a bumpy green pickle from the brine. Everyone called the aproned cashier Mamma. Mamma nodded and smiled at her choice as she snapped open a white wax paper bag. "Don't spend it all in one place!" Mamma commanded, returning a quarter, dime and two nickels in change.

She could never wait until she got outside, but must crunch into the thing while still under the aromatic spell of the deli. Once she was in the daylight, mouth full, dabbing juice from her chin, she realized what she had done. Now they'd think she'd gone past on purpose to eat a garlicky old pickle before her haircut. She'd reek.

With great reluctance she set the pickle in the trash can on the corner and wiped her fingers on her red dungarees. A bent old woman in black coat, black shoes and black babushka *tsked* as she passed. Ericka had one left of a two-pack of Chicklets her father had brought her from the subway and she cracked its white coating to get the mint in her mouth. She was going to do this.

Where once the heavily accented, hair-greased man who had owned the Mala Strana Salon had swept the sidewalk, now each morning as she passed on her way to school she saw a woman sweeping. Another woman often went in and out. One Sunday morning the second woman washed the plate glass window, loudly whistling "There Is Nothing Like A Dame" as she stretched to reach the top of the arch of brand new gold letters that spelled Snip'N'Shape. She'd been impressed by the whistler's brisk thoroughness and by her hair cut, kind of swept back, with a dip in front, and shaped to a point on the neck. No feathering. No prettying up. Her mother would hate it.

The sign in the window that said *NO APPOINTMENT NECESSARY* was still there. She pushed the door open, eyes to the worn maroon linoleum floor. The shop smelled just as bad as the Elegante. Dark nylons and white shoes appeared in front of her. She looked up. The beautician, just her height, wore a tight white uniform and held out her arms, hands open, as if Ericka were a long lost friend.

"Hi, honey. Here for a cut?"

Ericka felt her breath stop. The woman's long, narrow eyes were dark as semisweet chocolate and welcoming under angular eyebrows. Her nose was sharply yet elegantly curved, her dusky-brown hair so waved it looked ruffled. Her broad, keenly-etched lips smiled, dressed up in a grapey lipstick. Ericka looked quickly away when she noticed that behind the hairdresser a row of three ladies under silver space-helmet driers stared past magazines at them, cigarettes between index and middle fingers. Another beautician, this one very tall, bent over a sink and scrubbed an old woman's white hair. Ericka saw no sign of the whistling woman who washed windows like a proud shop owner.

The small beautician was never still. She swung a stiff transparent cape over her as soon as Ericka was seated, then sprayed her head wet with an excess of movement that made a performance of her attentions. "Like this again?" she asked, holding up a hank of overgrown pixie hair. She smelled of a kind of flowery powder that Ericka's mother patted on with an oversized puff. Did she cut the whistling window washer's hair? Ericka's insides quivered.

She got chills as the beautician, warm-fingered, refastened the cape at the nape of her neck. Her heart worked like a bongo drum as she answered, "No."

"Like what?"

She had nothing but the picture in her mind of the whistler. They must be very good friends to go in on a shop together. While Ericka searched for words the beautician bent down so they were virtually cheek to cheek in the mirror and asked, "What's your name, honey?"

She had practiced this three hundred times before her mirror. She'd put herself to sleep chanting it. Erickas were blonde, and tall, and swam like fish, rode with men in sports cars, wore cocktail dresses and used those huge powder puffs. "Rickie," she announced.

"Say that again?"

She was so used to whispering it. "Rickie," she barked, then cleared her throat to show that she hadn't meant to be abrupt. "Rickie Deigh."

The door opened and the whistling window washer strode in, hands in her pockets. "Angela," she said, in a bark of her own, and waited by the register.

"Tam!" called the beautician. She turned back to Rickie. "Do you want to look at some photographs I have of hairstyles, honey?" Angela gave her an album of eight by ten black and white portraits, then patted her own ruffled hair and sped to the desk.

Glamour pusses, she thought, flipping pages. Not for her the bouffant, the permanent wave. She lingered over a petite model so pretty she couldn't bear to turn the page. In the mirror Angela listened to the whistler. Rickie studied Tam's trim, jaunty haircut as the woman flung out her arms. Their voices got louder in the roar of the driers.

"Thirty days," Tam said. "We get it paid up in a month or we're up the creek without a paddle."

"You can't work two jobs and keep this place up, Tam." Angela spoke quickly, in the barbed way of New Yorkers, but there was a syrupy quality to her voice, as if it came from some rich source in her throat. "Give it time. We're getting more customers every day." Angela indicated Rickie with the flutter of a hand. Rickie wrenched her eyes down to the pretty model, but back up in time to see Tam looking her way.

Rickie burned with a second-degree blush. Tam looked like herself, in her dreams. Angela might be the friend Rickie danced with, in her dreams.

Tam shook her head. Her voice was not high, but not like a man's either. It was subdued, strong. Rickie wondered if she could find a voice like that in herself and quietly cleared her throat, lowered her chin. Tam announced, "I'm going to take the job. Till we get over the hump."

Angela, semi-sweet eyes pleading, stood very still and whispered, "But I'll never get to see you, hon."

Rickie would keep Angela company! She could sweep and wash windows. Put up advertisements all over town. How often could she get her hair cut? Across Cannon Street a truck ground to a stop, idled. It drowned out Angela and Tam. If she had a million dollars, she imagined, she'd bow and present it to Angela. *You've saved the shop!* Instead of studying

41

haircuts, she dreamed. Angela so grateful she took Rickie's hands. Rickie would crack some joke, draw himself up full, then gently, then firmly, press a hand to Angela's back, lift her delicate arm, and, under a velvety starlit night, dance her down Cannon Street.

Angela, darting back, startled her. "Find anything you like?"

Tongue-tied still, she stared at Angela in the mirror. She was dizzy. Stiff as a wooden dummy, she handed Angela the album. "I don't want to look like them," she said, her voice uncontrollably loud in her effort to lower it to Tam's timbre. Tam looked up. "I want to look like her."

In the mirror, she watched Angela follow her pointing finger to Tam. Angela's whole face changed, eyebrows lifting, eyes widening, mouth going round with an "Oh," only Rickie could hear.

Angela's hands on her hair were like lacy warm waterfalls. Each time Angela touched the back of her neck, Rickie shuddered like she did at the feel of the delicious warmth of her blankets these chilly nights. What was going on? From her heart down she was molten. Whenever hair was not falling into her eyes she watched Angela's face in the mirror. Angela had a grown-up flirtiness to her. Her hands did not seem to move so much as beckon. Her eyes, checking her work, kept smiling a knowing smile at Rickie. Her fingertips brushed hair off Rickie's cheekbone, forehead. Sometimes Angela's soft belly pressed fleetingly against a shoulder. Rickie felt like she would explode, like at night, when she practiced with her pillow how to kiss.

She was about to soar away, but at the same time, sat more and more still for Angela's deft touches, and feared that Angela could see her heat waves, like the ones that rose off the asphalt ahead of her when she roller-skated to Cannon Street on a hot summer day. And if Angela did notice? Would Angela laugh, keep cutting, keep touching, keep her soaring and sitting happily ever after?

Tam stood at the window flipping through a magazine. Lucky Tam. Did she and Angela go home to one of those new buildings down off Main Street? What if she, not Tam, lived with Angela, in a big sunny apartment with acres of shiny floors and big potted plants to dance around. What if she lived with Angela in a place where at night they could see the whole city sparkling like diamond rings. What if they went to the park together, tulips awakening at their feet as they walked around the lake, holding hands. And what if sometimes Angela waited for her outside school for everyone to see. Or if Angela fixed her hair every day, fingers swift and sure and attentive, like this.

Then it was over, the gentle fingers withdrawn, Angela's snipping dance done, the lusciously cloying scent of her powder removed. She gulped air.

"What do you think, Rickie?"

It was the first time she'd heard her name from other lips. She stared in the mirror and saw nothing but Angela's big tender smile. "I love it," she managed to say in a high strangled voice.

Angela clucked with her tongue and swung her around in the chair. "Tam. Show time."

Tam had a faint swagger in her walk, like a movie

cowboy. She approached slowly, leaned her arms on the back of the next chair. "Hot stuff," she pronounced in that murmur of a voice.

Tam was teasing her. She couldn't bear the humiliation in front of Angela and swept the cape from her chest.

Angela put a light hand on Rickie's shoulder and Rickie leaned into it, just enough to memorize the touch. "Come back in a month, six weeks, Rickie. We'll work on it some more, get it just right. You'll be irresistible."

She caught the affectionate smile between Angela and Tam, slid off the chair, started for the door feeling mad, feeling pleased, weak from imagined passion, not knowing what she felt.

"Oops," she said and whirled back around, pointedly not looking at Tam, searching her pockets. Into Angela's soft hand she carefully lay her mother's money, along with her own quarter, dime and two nickels. "Thanks," she coughed out, making it to the door, then stumbling on the welcome mat as she glanced back and saw that Angela's warm gaze followed her.

Cannon Street, her avenue of dreams, throbbed with clamorous possibility. The daylight dazzled her, the fumes of a passing bus were the offering of a rose garden. She peered toward the cannon, cocked an ear for its salute, noticed that the sidewalk had receded far below her and that everyone had Angela's smile.

"Come back," Angela had said.

She mooned over the florist's window, giddily pleased to have nothing left in her pockets but her hands. Cool air touched the new bare place on her neck. In the florist's window she saw Angela's touch, her hair kind of swept back, with a dip in front. She felt the cowboy swagger in her own walk.

THE NIGHT QUEEN

"We should forget breakfast and go straight home to bandage them," I say. I was too hot and tired for any more trouble that night.

"Nah. This is nothing," Merle tells me, sucking on the knuckles of her right hand, one by one. She cleans the blood from the broken skin on each and every finger, and by the time she's through, the first one's red again.

"You need some iodine," Callie says. "Right, Flo?"

Flo has dimples as big as her eyes. She towers over the rest of us. "What she needed was to let her buddy in on the action, baby," she announces in her foghorn voice. "If Callie and me hadn't of been making out in the can, we would of creamed the SOB, Merle."

"Merle did enough damage," I say, trying not to nag. I squiggle around a little next to Merle, look over my black-and-white checked suit. Small checks. I usually wear it to work at the elementary school office, but it goes good with the sheer blouse Merle likes because it kind of shows that mole right over my bra. Lord, it was hot that night. Even with the diner door open and the floor fans going, I could feel a puddle of sweat inside the bra.

Merle's got her sleeves rolled up to her forearms, jean jacket on a hook. Her hair's sand-brown and brushed straight back from her forehead. Her eyebrows slant up over her nose so she always looks a little bit put out, like nobody wants to answer some hard question she asked. "That loser was after my woman, what do you want?"

I love when she calls me her woman, how she doesn't have any question at all about how it is between us. Too quick for anyone in the diner to see, I dart an arm through hers and squeeze close, then scoot away and fluff up my hair, like that's all I was doing in the first place. I tease it up so I look taller. "I just hate you getting hurt is all, Merle."

Slouched down in the booth, Merle's no bigger than me, but never tell her that. She's watching her knuckles bleed, sneering like Elvis. "I hated her making a play for you, Tiny. Friggin' Upton bulldaggers."

"They're the worst," Flo agrees.

Callie's hair is just beauty-parlor straightened. She

had a reddish tint put in this time. She uses the menu she's been fanning herself with to slap at Flo. "You just don't like my ex from Upton."

"Ain't that the truth."

I laugh, but not hard, so my eyes don't get like little slits. It takes a good makeup job to make them look bigger as it is. "What's a girl to do? Morton River's not exactly Provincetown. You and me grabbed the most eligible butches in the Valley, Cal."

"Merle's face is bleeding again."

"Ohh," I can't help saying. I grab napkins from the shiny metal holder and dip them in my water glass, pushing the paper compress at Merle.

"Thanks, doc," she says. She pushes back the hair she's always combing into a sideburn and presses the wet wad of paper to her cheekbone where it's going dark. "I think she had brass knuckles."

I wince. It's almost like I can feel the cold napkins on my face.

"She knew she needed something, coming up against you," Flo tells her. Those dimples make Flo look good-natured even when she tries to be as tough as Merle. Which she always tries.

Merle rolls her jaw back and forth. I'm hoping she didn't chip any teeth. We finally paid off the dentist bill last month.

This is at the Night Queen on our way home from the River's Edge Tavern. Stopping at the Queen, drinking at the Edge, walking home in the early A.M. are rituals on the weekends when Merle and Flo don't have overtime. They both run machines at the spring factory, do setup and maintenance and whatever else the bosses can make them do without paying them extra.

Merle shrugs, sets the napkins down and leans back, folding her arms across her chest, eyebrows up again, but this time her eyes are laughing at us. When she looks straight at someone, her eyes are amber, I swear, like light's coming through from behind. One glimpse and I always feel like it's the first night all over again.

"What the hell," Merle says, holding out her scarred hands for us to see, napkins and all. "These mitts are always a mess from those damn wild coils anyway."

"Tell me about it," Flo agrees, showing the calloused ruts along her fingertips. I always wonder how that feels to Callie. "Wire at those speeds," Flo says, sad, "is nobody's friend."

"It's a job," says Merle. She takes out her comb and fixes the backsweep of her hair. "Right, buddy?"

"Puts beans on the table," Flo agrees, poking an elbow at Callie. They laugh. Flo aims and swats a mosquito on Callie's arm.

"What's the joke?" I reach over to Merle with my stocking toes and rub her ankle. "They remind me of us, our first year."

Merle taps the ring on my third finger. "When are you two going to tie the knot?"

"Leave them alone, Merle. They're only what — three months?"

"Is that all?" asks Callie. Her wide eyes are like a kid's at a birthday party, the same look as when I get away from the office long enough to visit her in the school cafeteria where she works. I didn't see much of Callie after she dropped out of high school to get married, didn't even know I missed her, but looking back, I can see that I was always trying to find another best friend just like her.

Foghorn Flo says, "It feels like we're about to have our golden wedding anniversary!"

"Shh," I whisper, quick. They're forgetting that we're not at the Edge.

"To hell with the squares." Merle's all sulky again, hiding underneath her eyelids, muttering so low I can hardly hear her over the floor fans.

The waitress brings breakfast.

"Must be morning!" says Flo, like always.

And Callie always grabs Flo's wrist, looks at her watch, then delivers her line. "It is morning!"

We all laugh.

Merle slathers grape jelly on her toast, then swirls more jelly around in her eggs like ketchup. She never fails to eat like a horse after a fight.

"You boys be good," I tell our beaus after we're full. I slip my sandals back on. "I'm fixing my face, Callie."

This is a very good part of the night, when me and Callie squeeze into the ladies for a quick pee and face repair before we walk home.

"I guess Merle showed that one what for," Callie says from behind the pumpkin-colored bathroom stall. "You could drown in the Lysol in here."

"Mmm," I answer, giving my lips little pops to spread the lipstick. Pink. I don't go for the hot reds anymore. They make me look like an over-the-hill lady of the night. I get up on my tiptoes and bend over the sink to get a good look in the clouded mirror. The porcelain sink, curved like a hip against me, is cool. Soon, soon me and Merle can get under our cool sheets.

"I don't understand why it always happens to you, Tiny. I mean, not that you're not dynamite to look at, but what do you do, lead them on?"

Twenty years ago in high school Callie and me used to pretend we were boy and girl making out — for practice. I've learned a few things since then. Callie still has a lot to learn.

"You know I don't."

"Then does Merle do something to get their goat?"

"Yeah. She exists." I let Callie have the sink. "She's top dog in Morton River. These Upton types come up here slumming and strutting, thinking the hicks are going to swoon at their feet. They have another think coming when they run into Merle." I go in to use the toilet and call over the stall, "Not that I can't take care of myself. I think she does it to save her honor — not mine."

"What do you mean, girl?"

I stretch over for the last pieces of toilet paper on the roll. A lot of the nail polish graffiti is gay: Ronnie'n'Doris, Lisa'n'Al, F and C Forever — Flo and Callie can't write out two female-sounding names.

"Where else can she be king of the roost?" I ask.

"Home with you?"

A *lot* to learn. I say nothing, just bend to straighten the seams in my nylons.

"Flo says she's top producer at work."

"That means a ton in a man's job, doesn't it?" I say, slamming the stall door open and marching to the sink. "She still gets paid a dollar an hour less than the men, plus she's wrecking her body proving herself all the time. All the time." I don't say this to Callie, but it used to be that Merle made love to me all day Sundays. Now Merle soaks in the tub and lets me rub her back.

Merle and Flo are at the register when we finish, chitchatting with the waitress Merle used to date. Merle takes a toothpick and flicks it around on her tongue till it falls into just the right spot in a corner of her mouth. She slings her jean jacket over her shoulder.

"Get the lead out, girls," she tells us in that take-charge way of hers. I can't help a glimpse back at that poor waitress who didn't know enough to hang onto Merle.

"What do you two do in the little girls' room," Flo asks when we're out on Railroad Avenue again, "clean the place?"

"It needs it," Callie says, laughing that high clear laugh of hers, like a glass wind chime, so I think they can hear it in the houses on top of the Hillside.

The moon's so bright it lights up the windows of the old brick factories across the street. There's no traffic at this hour. Only the running river reminds me the four of us aren't alone in the world. A damp breeze finds us. Merle shrugs into her jacket.

"Is your kid home tonight?" Flo's whispering in her foghorn voice. She thinks we can't hear.

"Yeah," Callie whispers back. "Your folks?"

"They're going up the river tomorrow, but it's still too cold to sleep in their little cabin."

"I wish you could stay the night. You'll walk me home?"

"Oh yeah, baby. I'll walk you to the ends of the earth."

"I wish we could at least hold hands."

"How about —" They're rustling all the way across Main Street. "It's nobody's business what's in your pocket!" says Callie and sounds her chime laugh again. The heat from the two of them comes barreling along the sidewalk at us like a steamroller.

I suck in a deep breath. "You could take the couch, Merle," I whisper, trying to be fairy godmother to the new couple. "I'd sleep on the old daybed your mother gave you."

Merle flicks her toothpick to the other side, eases her hands into her slash pockets, thinks it over. I hope she's remembering how Tiger and Marjorie — Tiger's dead now, from the emphysema, and I visit Marjorie in the nursing home, but she doesn't know me anymore — used to let us have their place for a few hours on Saturday nights while they went to the movies.

Finally Merle says, "They've got it bad." She turns on a dime. "Hey, you two lovebirds," she says, walking backwards.

Flo and Callie's hands fly out of Flo's pocket. "Nothing like scaring the pants off us."

Merle cocks her head and brags from the side of her mouth, "I never had to scare them off a woman yet." I have to swallow a laugh. If I didn't love my little butch like I do I'd think she was too much. She spits the toothpick out. "Ask them," she says to me, turning back.

It's not an order. Merle gets gruff when she's feeling shy. I say, "Why don't you two come over to our place for the night? You can have the bedroom."

It's like Lucy and Ethel the way their mouths fall open at the same second. Lucy and Ethel if somebody just told them it's okay to jump each other's bones right there and then.

Then Callie groans. "I can't leave my kid all night. She's seventeen, so a few hours are okay, but what kind of example is that, not to come home at all?"

Flo's face falls. "*When* are we going to get a night together, baby?"

"I can't just not go home, Flo. It wouldn't be right. She'd think I don't care about her. I might have been married at her age, but inside I was a little girl still."

Flo nods. "You're right. You're a hell of a lot better mom than I ever had. I'm not used to it. Come on, you two, stop getting our hopes up. Anyway, the kid won't be home all tomorrow afternoon."

I tease them: "Remind me not to call Callie's place tomorrow!"

"Aw," says Flo.

Callie stuffs her hand back in Flo's pocket. "Don't be embarrassed, they do it too."

"Who says?" Merle asks quick, giving her crooked smile, the one that shows her missing tooth.

Callie gets me back. "I know Tiny!"

"Hey," says Flo, "I've got a new elephant joke. Why do elephants have wrinkled knees?"

"Because their nylons are sagging," says Callie, yanking at hers.

"No! From playing marbles!"

We all groan like we're supposed to at Flo's corny riddles, then we tell more jokes, clown around, hush for the long steep climb past the dark houses. A dog-day cicada rattles off its heat alarm, but all's well with my world. Its like we're in a moonlit bubble of content. Didn't we have jobs? Didn't me and Merle have seven whole years together? Weren't Flo and Callie brand spanking new, like birthday presents to each other? Life really is good.

Merle brushes a hand across my back like she's flicking off a bug or something, but I know, in a better world, she'd be putting her arm around me.

Then Callie yelps, real loud into the dead silent night. Something falls at her feet. She's staggering, falls against Flo. There's a stream of blood down Callie's face.

"What the —"

"Where —"

"Run!"

"I can't! I've got Callie. Baby! Are you okay?" Flo whispers.

Callie straightens. "Ohhh," she wails.

This stuff happens and I turn into an animal, all ears, wanting only to run like hell, but it's Callie. "Can you walk?"

Another rock slashes by and hits the hedge behind us.

"I'm not staying around here!" Callie sobs and shuffles up the narrow sidewalk.

"Fuckin' lezzies!" comes a male voice. Other men laugh, young from the sound. Men without women on a Saturday night.

Merle's like a pointer dog. "Come on," I tell her.

But she yells, "Where the hell are you, scum? Show your ugly faces!"

"What're *you* going to do to us, runty lez? Huh?"

"They're kids, Merle. Don't let them get to you." My voice sounds to me like I'm talking along a quivering string between tin cans.

Merle pulls away. She kicks at a tree stump with her square-toed boots like it's the whole communist army. Only, I'm thinking, we don't need to go to Russia to find trouble.

"You're not at the Edge, Merle," I tell her, attaching to her arm. Her body is tight as a scream you have to swallow. "You can't protect us. This is dangerous."

Merle pushes away from me. "I'm *sick* of this crap. Go on home."

Just like that I'm not scared anymore, only icy cold all the way through. Pressing my purse so tight against my chest I hurt, I say, "I am not leaving your side."

Nothing happens for so long it's like the Twilight Zone. I'm meantime smelling the cut grass in the yard behind us. Someone, say while I was fixing our coldcut supper, was mowing a lawn in the twilight, listening to the kids call back and forth playing street hockey, racing tricycles. Then maybe the mower stopped and someone struck a match to a cigarette, smelled the sulphur, watched the light fade, heard screen doors slam and the last jingle of the ice cream truck, just at dark.

A hoodlum smashes a bottle. Four of them step off the porch of a three-story house. In the moonlight I can make out moss growing between the shingles. One man makes wet-sounding kissing noises. "That your *girl*-friend there, lesbo? Give her to us, we'll show her a good time."

"Merle," I plead, "Merle, come home."

Merle pulls away. She starts toward the men, striking the metal taps of her heels extra loud on the cement. I catch at her sleeve. The four men talk about what they'll do to me. Merle strips off her jacket. She lurches toward them, chin up high, letting loose a stream of curses like a growl.

Flo comes out of nowhere and grabs Merle's arm, jerking her back. I've still got hold of the jean jacket and grab her wrist. Together we walk Merle a step backwards, away from the men.

"I thought you wanted in on the action, *buddy*," Merle taunts Flo.

"Callie might need a doctor," Flo says, voice forceful though her face is sick-pale. "We need your phone to call a cab, Merle."

"Take them home, Tiny."

"Don't be stupid. Not without you."

"Come here, bulldyke! We'll be glad to give you a turn. *After* we get through with your girlfriend." Their laughter is like chalk on a blackboard. I feel the hairs on my neck shiver.

"Merle!" It's all we can do to keep dragging her. Merle's arm is damp with sweat. She strains forward.

"They can't get away with this," she's saying, her voice like a file, hiding tears. She's too slight for Flo's bulky strength and knows she's losing ground. "Don't you get it? I couldn't ever show my face again!"

From an open window someone screams, "Shut up, I'm calling the cops!" Another window slams down. The men laugh and strut back to their porch. Merle lets herself be wrestled over to the tree stump, shakes us off, then leads us farther up the hill to where Callie is moaning on someone's chipped flagstone steps.

"How I'm going to explain this to my kid?" Callie asks, holding up her bloody hanky.

Merle snaps her fingers over her shoulder, like it's all behind us now. "Come on. Flo, don't let her just sit there."

They ease Callie up. Me, I'm like a dishrag by this time. It's quiet again. Nothing is moving but the three of them hobbling ahead of me in the moonlight, like a refugee family fleeing without its belongings. I can hardly keep up.

At the top of the hill they turn into our alleyway. In the backyard I see that the upstairs neighbor left limp white sheets on the line all night. The squeal of the pulley bringing them in will wake us to the bright hot day.

Inside we can see Callie better. The bleeding's stopped. I'm so tired, and so glad to see home, smell home, be safe home. I clean Callie up in my bathroom, replacing her blouse with a towel just like in high school, when we fixed each other's hair.

"That rock must have hit a vein or something," I tell her, sponging the wound. She bites her lip at every touch. "You've got a good bump too."

"I don't want to go to the emergency," Callie says. "I *won't,* so don't tell me I need to. I've got to get home."

There'd be too many questions, names. What if a cop was hanging around? "I don't think you need stitches, Cal. You feel dizzy or anything?"

"No, just a headache."

I scold. "That's from the last pitcher of beer."

Callie laughs, then groans and puts her hands to her head. "Exactly what it feels like."

"Okay, then. Put your shirt on. We'll get you home by cab."

"But Flo'll never take a cab from my place. Those

guys'll kill her. I'm so scared, Tiny." Callie presses herself against my middle, hooks her arms around my waist. "I'm going to miss our walks."

This tired, I can't help getting a little sharp. "You think this will keep Merle home?"

"Oh." She pulls away, looks up in surprise. "I wish I could hide here with you two forever."

After the cab leaves, after all the lights are out but the moon, Merle and me squeeze under the covers in her twin bed. Merle's pajama top is open. I find a soft white breast, lay my lips on it. Here, not far from the reservoir, the tree frogs throb.

I shiver under the soft cool sheets, and press closer to Merle who feels hot as a falling star. A passing car, revving its engine, makes me ask, "You don't think they followed us?"

Merle, stiff, doesn't answer. A long freight train calls a warning at each crossing, over and over.

"I kept looking back," I whisper into Merle's breast, "and I didn't see them. Do you think they could tell Flo and Callie were holding hands? Did they do it because Callie's not white?"

Merle is quiet as the grave. Her sideburns look like spit curls now, her neck and shoulders are all creamy woman, asking for caresses.

"Merle." No answer. "You asleep?" I don't even know if she's breathing. I go cold again with stark terror. Have they killed her somehow? I prop myself on my elbows and in the dark stare down at her. "Merle!"

Then she folds in on me, like Callie did, her back heaving, face running with tears, her poor scarred hands wringing the life out of the bedclothes.

"Ohh, baby," I say, putting my arms around Merle

and pulling her magnificent head against the opening in my nightgown. But I can't hold Merle as close as I want, as I need. Her pride's too tender. I can only sing, "I love you, I love you, I love you," until her storm subsides into a sound like the train's.

She looks up at me, eyebrows in their question mark, asking the things she'll always be too proud to admit not knowing. Voice gruff, she says, "I'm not scared."

I hold her as tight as I dare, dreading the fight she'll find next week at the Edge.

THE BIG BAD WOLF
Jefferson 5

Jefferson paced under the hotel canopy. She moved away from the gray building, out to the curb, back along the red mat to the glass double doors. The doorman, about sixty, whose uniform sported golden-brown shoulder braids which almost matched his skin, watched her with a scowl on his face. At first, she'd explained that she was waiting for a guest. That had been half an hour ago, when she was fifteen minutes early. Now she scowled back at him.

What was he going to do? Call the cops because she wanted to make amends to Shirley and was just a little bit anxious?

She looked quickly up, but it was only a family leaving the hotel. The sharp scent of the father's lime aftershave hung behind him in the wet air. A tiny girl in a hooded red rain cape held his hand. He lifted the little girl over the water in the gutter and set her in a waiting limousine next to her mother, then waved until they were out of sight.

Jefferson recombed her wet hair. "Amends, Jefferson," she told herself. "You're making amends to the woman, not seducing her all over again." Then why had she put on cologne? Why the new burgundy shirt she'd been saving for a special occasion? Why her favorite cracked and faded brown leather jacket, and her softest cords? Why was her heart doing the tango, double time, inside her chest?

Again, activity in the lobby. Again, it was not Shirley. What would she look like after ten years on the West Coast, writing comedy in movieland? Would she be harried like some of the L.A. career women Jefferson had met? Or just her zany old self, cracking jokes with every breath, unable to relax even long enough to make love decently, despite having come on like a hurricane, despite acting like a mini-sex goddess. Why in hell had Jefferson been obsessed with getting the woman to bed?

Because that's how she'd been in those days here in New York. It hadn't just been Shirley, it had been a host of women that Jefferson had pursued from age sixteen on, with a frenzy that had given her no rest. And for what? What was left? Not even good memories. When it had come time to sort through what she'd done, and to whom, she'd found that the histories of all those beloveds, not to mention the details of the relationships, eluded her in a way the women never could. Now she was tracking every one of them down. She had to clean up yesterday to make today work.

Damn. Where was Shirley? It was half an hour past their meeting time. Jefferson felt clammy, chilled through. Did she get the day wrong? The time? The hotel? Should she go up?

No. That was the last thing she was going to do. She'd already spotted a coffee shop around the corner where they could talk safely. She'd even purposely left her big black umbrella at home, the one she'd used so often as an excuse to pull a woman near for the first time. Had she used the umbrella with Shirley? Would Shirley be expecting it? In any case, she herself would not fall into any of the traps she'd set for others.

For a moment, Jefferson stopped pacing. She stood at the edge of the canopy, peering through the downpour at the yellow cabs, the black cabs, the mail jeeps, the limos, the beat-up economy cars that jammed Broadway at the end of this crosstown street. Rain seemed to trap the exhaust smells. A few people with umbrellas squeezed through the gridlock, then turned up Broadway at a furious pace, as if to make up for lost time.

Lost time. Jefferson jammed her hands back in her pockets and whirled into her pacing again. Forty years she'd lost in her games of sodden pursuit. Because it was true, what Ginger had said, that as soon as Jefferson had stopped drinking, she had also stopped whoring around. And Ginger ought to know.

She'd been the woman left at home, left without a whole lover, or just plain left, for the majority of those years.

What could they have had if Jefferson had stayed home? A little of the peace she sometimes experienced now? A feeling of freedom, like she could do anything, go anywhere and it would be good, without fighting or tears or conflict? Without the feeling that some malevolent creature lived inside her and busied itself tearing her up, so that everything took a hundred times more effort because first she had to stitch herself back together again?

Jefferson took her hands out of their hiding places. She stood, half under the side of the canopy, half in the rain, looking at them. First the backs, pale and chafed from the long winter. Then the palms, callused a little from working out recently. Her right palm collected rain in a tiny puddle at its center. These were the hands that had stopped dragging themselves, one over the other, up an endless rough rope. She licked the rainwater in her palm. Its taste was metallic, almost bitter, and snapped her right into the present, into this moment of waiting to make another apology for being such a creep in the past.

A cab pulled in front of the hotel so quickly that Jefferson surmised it had been stuck in the Broadway traffic. Without seeming to move, the doorman was beside it, sweeping the passenger door open. A leg appeared, high-heeled shoe first, then a long calf with the edge of a dark clinging skirt at its peak.

L.A. had been good to Shirley. Jefferson smelled her own sweat and felt the tango begin again. Had

Shirley changed so much, or had Jefferson just forgotten the poise, the warm smile, the arms that hugged as if they were made for welcoming back old lovers. Didn't Shirley remember how Jefferson had dumped her, abandoned her in that sleazy bar for a quickie with a woman she'd had her eye on for weeks, and who'd finally returned Jefferson's interest that night? She couldn't hug Shirley back, so consumed was she by the old guilt.

"Come on up, handsome. The years have seasoned you nicely," said Shirley, offering her arm.

Jefferson didn't so much hear and see as feel the cab pull away, leaving a vacuum she suddenly had to fill. Instead of being in the hotel waiting for their meeting, Shirley had been out living her own life and caught Jefferson off balance. And she hadn't expected Shirley to have this presence, this woman-of-the-world air of command.

"Jefferson?" Shirley said after a moment.

Quickly, Jefferson answered, "I thought we could go to the coffee shop around the corner."

"Oh, God, Jeff. I am wiped, I have to use the little girls' room, and I long to change out of this monkey suit. You can wait in the lobby if you want, but I promise not to bite." The doorman was watching the sky, hands behind his back. Jefferson felt like she was at the tail end of a tug of war, pulled forward under the canopy by a need to put an end to a past that shamed her, pulled back by temptations of repeating that past. In the few seconds she took to make a decision, she watched Shirley's face take on a look of concern, the doorman's, one of even deeper suspicion.

"Jefferson?" Shirley asked after a moment.

Jefferson took Shirley's arm and steered her into the lobby.

It was hot in there and smelled like the steam heat of old New York buildings. As they crossed the lobby she could see herself, Shirley's elbow cupped in her hand, in a mirror. The floor was a huge shiny black and white checkerboard and Shirley's heels clicked across it.

"What's the story, handsome?" Shirley asked. "This isn't *kid*napping at my age, you know."

Jefferson managed a smile. They sat facing each other on a faded couch. Cream-painted columns dotted the lobby like elderly guests half-snoozing the afternoon away.

The feel of Shirley's arm, grown more substantial over the years, still burned against Jefferson's palm. She had always touched women like lovers, she realized. It was as much second nature to her as worrying about how she looked. Was it too late to learn how to be friends?

"Do you mind if we don't go upstairs?"

"Since when is Jefferson afraid of the big bad wolf?" asked Shirley.

"Aw, hell, Shirley," she answered. "That's just the problem. I *am* the big bad wolf. If I went up there with you I might act like I used to and that's not what I want." She felt about as debonair and in control of this situation as the three little pigs.

"What *do* you want, Jeffers?"

Now she remembered what had sparked her desire for Shirley. Those vivid blue eyes, like a splash of cold water, a surprise every time. Just as she always had, Jefferson stared into them, withdrew from their intimacy, but went back for more. She leaned into the couch and let her hands crawl inside her pants pockets where she fingered a heart-shaped stone Ginger had found on the beach during their second honeymoon, after Ginger had taken Jefferson back yet again.

"I want to apologize."

The blue eyes looked shocked. "For what?" asked Shirley. "For being the prettiest butch I ever beguiled into my bed?"

"*You* beguiled me into *your* bed?" It had never occurred to Jefferson that the campaign might have been mutual.

Shirley lifted wavy hair back from her eyes. "Don't you remember? I interrupted the great chase. You wanted what's-her-name, that siren everybody was after. What was her name?"

"Cindy?" Jefferson asked, not really sure herself.

"Yes! And the last time you and I went out together — well, you got drunk again and I decided Cindy could have you. So what are you apologizing for?"

Jefferson sat straight up and ran her fingers through her hair. Shirley had let her go? "I'm apologizing for disappearing on you at the bar. For going off with Cindy."

Shirley was still toying with her own hair. She shrugged. "That's the way it was back then. Or the way I was. Trying out this one and that one. Not that you didn't measure up the nights we spent together." Shirley looked up into Jefferson's face from under her hair, her laugh like melting chocolate.

Jefferson struggled to get out of the past, the bar, the guilt of having abandoned this woman. "What did you do?"

Shirley narrowed her eyes and cocked her head. "Are you serious? What do you think I did? We did?"

"Not the nights we spent together. After I left you. In the bar."

"Actually, I think I'd rather describe our nights together. But who can remember any of it? Why?"

Jefferson pulled herself back on track. "Because I need to apologize for a lot of things. It's part of getting well for me."

Shirley relaxed against the couch now and seemed to study Jefferson. "Okay," she said after a while. "Thanks. I appreciate you caring after all these years." She smiled. "I like you better this way, you know. Undrunk."

Nodding, Jefferson smiled. "Yes. Me too."

Shirley reached over and ruffled Jefferson's hair. "You look like a drowned rat. You want to come up and dry off, big bad wolf? My promise still holds."

"Your promise?"

"That I won't bite."

Jefferson took a deep breath. The tug of war had started again. Couldn't she just spend some time getting acquainted with this woman she obviously didn't know at all? She almost pulled her comb from her pocket, but stopped herself. How she looked didn't matter. "Okay."

"Good," Shirley replied, standing and starting toward the elevator.

Jefferson watched her, her hips, from across the checkerboard floor. The rain still poured loudly down outside the windows on the other side of the lobby.

Shirley whirled at the elevator, cocked a hand on her hip as if presenting herself for Jefferson's inspection and asked, "Because tell me the truth, Jeffers, am I *really* your typical Red Riding Hood type?"

She remembered that tiny girl in the red cape who'd come out of the hotel earlier. She laughed, shaking her head. "No, you're not. But I liked being the big bad wolf so much I thought you were." She joined Shirley and, as the elevator lifted them, could almost see the old wolf in the lobby below, waving goodbye.

THE FIRES OF WINTER SOLSTICE

The fire, thought LilyAnn Lee, who was six feet tall even without her fire fighters' boots, could have been worse. A big old warehouse full of furniture, an alert little watchman who'd smelled the smoke despite the flask in his pocket.

It had been clear to her right away, from the smell and pattern, that the fire was electrical in origin, so as soon as they'd controlled the flames, they began the tedious job of finding where it had started, and making certain it spread no further. This was the kind of work that demanded only half of LilyAnn's mind. She drifted above the garbagey wet smoke smell, above the splintered furniture, above her light on the wall as she excavated for signs of burning wiring.

Now and then a distinct whiff of burnt cedar reached her from that stack of hope chests she and Horrigan had wet down for fear of sparks. A smell like the cedar they'd burned in Alley Pond Park last year for the Solstice Ritual. Her friends from the Women's Food Co-op had been urging her to return this year, but damn, she'd been so uncomfortable.

All those white girls, she thought, those earnest women with their dead-serious incantation of the Goddess. There was something so thin and pale about their very ceremony. They gathered in circles like doubting but hopeful supplicants who prayed extra hard to get past a sense of make-believe. The woman who'd learned rituals on the west coast seemed intense and desperate, determined to perform her office exactly right, not to let any wavering spirit she called on flee in the tendrils of smoke that rose from the tiny illicit fire in the park. She wondered if Dawn and Goldie, the other sisters who'd been there, felt strange too. Would they go back into the night to sit in this year's cold circle?

She remembered, as she worked along the wall and checked periodically on big beefy Horrigan across from her, the promise of light in the women's song.

> *You can't kill the spirit*
> *She's like a mountain*

Bold and strong
She goes on and on.

It was getting smoky again. Had Horrigan found something? She couldn't see its source. She put her mask on, breathing easier, seeing somewhat better, and waved to Horrigan, who didn't seem bothered by the smoke yet and ignored her signal. He was a temporary partner, an old-timer whose regular partner, like hers, was on vacation. Horrigan was a bigot, but close enough to retirement not to buck this pairing with a black "fire impersonator," as he called the women in the department.

She peered through the smoke to the wires she followed. Upstairs more of the company searched, heavy-booted, as carefully as she. Sometimes she felt closer to these guys her life depended on than to the women at the Co-op. She partied with the women, sat in meetings with them, joined their ritual circles, but that click wasn't there, the click of bonding in the face of danger.

While she was drawn to women's spirituality, found it closer than anything else she could accept, it didn't *feel* anywhere as meaningful as the mass prayer at a fire fighter's funeral, or the firehouse Christmas tree. Didn't warm her even as much as the static-filled radio insistently filling their living quarters with carols. All the fire fighters, women and men, talked bah-humbug and complained about Christmas Day duty, but the women brought in baked goods, the guys gave out cartons of cigarettes or quarts of liquor.

LilyAnn had made a ritual of reporting for her

Christmas shift early with four uncooked mince pies and cooking them right there, filling the firehouse with their smell. Last year a false alarm had come in while they baked. LilyAnn had forgotten the pies until the truck was halfway back to the firehouse. She'd raced up to the oven. Someone had carefully gauged when the pies were done and turned the oven off, but she'd never been able to find out who.

She was chanting to herself as she worked.

> *You can't kill the spirit*
> *She's like a mountain*
> *Bold and strong*
> *She goes on and on.*

Her back ached from holding her arms up, the backs of her legs were beginning to tremble from the strain of walking sideways in a crouch, the mask was biting into her face, which had swelled from the heat.

She worked methodically on. Crazy things happened in these old buildings: fire just waiting to explode out of a wall where it was trapped, beams so weak the heat and water sent them crashing through the ceiling below. Horrigan was masked now too — professional, thorough, like her. He'd probably dragged many a black woman from a burning building. She hoped again that she could rely on him to rescue one more, even, she smiled to herself, if she was an unwelcome peer.

Unlike at Alley Pond where she, Goldie and Dawn were welcomed warmly, treated with respect, even wooed by the white women who'd learned that a healthy culture was an inclusive one. How the burnt cedar smell pulled her back to that night, helped her see that some part of herself longed for, belonged with the women as they lit their candles to light the way through whatever winter brought.

They'd used the cedar for purification, burned it carefully, with sentries posted, knowing full well that discovery meant more than a fine for their little bonfire surrounded by buckets of water. Celebrating the solstice was pagan; the police or the media could choose to make much of it. Were there still laws on the books against witchcraft?

Her rebellious self would return to the fire circle for certain. Hadn't her people, after all, been as defiant? They'd salvaged their African fires and chants, bits and pieces anyway, from the puritanical wrath they found on these shores. In the solstice circle she'd sat cross-legged, butt cold against the ground, feeling the souls of those ancestors swell and fill and heat her own body till she felt like a great Amazon warrior, one of many, many daughters of daughters, gargantuan and powerful. Was this fantasy or memory, she'd wondered. Hadn't the Amazons come from Africa, been darkskinned?

> *You can't kill the spirit*
> *She's like a mountain*
> *Bold and strong*
> *She goes on and on.*

The warehouse was silent but for the shuffling boots. She felt as if she were mining the world for light and heat, a lot more of both than the women's candles gave. The priestess had instructed each woman to light the candle of the woman to her left, and to address the topic of power when the light reached her. How they'd gather power to warm themselves, arm themselves against the frozen wasteland of the patriarchy.

Well, here I am, thought LilyAnn, working with that very patriarchal beast, sure hot enough now. Sweat ran down her face under the mask. She couldn't mop it with her fireretardant sleeve. Was the work making her hotter, or was she nearing a hidden fire?

She couldn't survive that African sun now, she decided. Her blood had changed. Where did she belong — the cold park, the hot warehouse, neither? The men stomped and chopped, getting noisy with frustration as they searched for fires that might not be there.

"You can't kill the spirit," the women had chanted. But even Goldie and Dawn had looked drawn and weak, and their voices had sounded quavery. Did LilyAnn want a spirit like she'd seen in church? One that would so move woman after woman that they'd flare into words or song and testify its strength? *Something,* anything but polite turn-taking, awk-wardly recited words. It seemed that she, along with the others, chipped and chipped away at the wall between them and their spirituality, bit by bit cut into the plaster that held them back.

Fire makes a sound like a great gulp when it finds enough oxygen to swallow. LilyAnn leapt back from the box-sized inferno that exploded at her. Her sweat was gone. Her training, like a blind faith, took her over. She quickly, distinctly, told her radio she needed help even as she turned to summon Horrigan. He'd heard the great gulp, though, and had begun his run across to her when another dreaded sound

78

filled her ears. A crack, a tearing, a "Whoa!" of surprise as Horrigan crashed through the floor.

So close to retirement, LilyAnn thought, and turned her back to the spreading flames. She ran along what she'd later picture as a wall of candles — the flames reflected in her mask's eyepiece — toward Horrigan who hung over the deep basement below. Cold air gusted up toward the flames, drawn like the fire fighters who she could hear rushing to contain them. She gave them the flames like gifts, trusting their skills.

Earlier she'd noted the placement of posts in the huge room and now ran to one, attached her rope, then treaded softly to the edges of the cold hole. She was big, but lighter than a running man. She prayed to the Goddess that the edge would hold as she lay, belly down, to crawl and stretch until she reached Horrigan.

> She's like a mountain
> Bold and strong
> She goes on and on

Damn, she thought as she attached the two rings which must hold Horrigan's weight, damn if that vision of herself as an Amazon didn't come back to make her feel trebly strong. And damn, she thought again as Horrigan heaved himself finally over the edge and they scuttled away from the weak floor — damn if that wall of candles wasn't there in her head to guide them through the thick smoke to safety.

They both grabbed hoses and helped drag them in, then trained them on the fire. The hoses were bonds she could see, linking them against danger. Yet the circle whose spirit she hadn't been able to see, touch, believe, had been there for her too, a song that moved with her, that moved her. She'd never expected to feel the joy that tingled everywhere inside her now in this rank-smelling fire site. And she'd never expected Horrigan's words, behind her on the hose.

"For a minute," he shouted, mask pushed aside, "I thought I might not be around this year to save your mince pies!"

Chant from *Like A Mountain* by Naomi Littlebear, Copyright Naomi Littlebear, 1977.

FRENCHY GOES TO VEGAS

There was no dark sky, there were no birds, no sight of moon or desert hills. There was only the water, cascading endlessly into pools under palms planted so regularly they looked unreal. And the fire. Flames that shot up with a roar, then down the falls and out into the water, coming closer and closer.

"EEEEEEE!" screamed a little girl, turning away from the rail. Her father lifted her and pressed her to his shoulder. She sobbed in terror, hiding her eyes. He laughed.

"Hey, that's something else," Frenchy said, not admitting to the twinge of uneasiness she felt too.

Gloria squeezed her hand under the cover of her cape. "I knew you'd like it, honey," she said.

"It's like being in Ben-Hur or, or —"

"It's exactly like being right where you are. Las Vegas. This whole place is one big show."

The fire receded to the original soaring flame and then that too disappeared. The excited babbling of the crowd replaced the roar. Frenchy checked and saw the little girl had dared to look. She pulled her father's hand. "Come on, Daddy, before it comes back!"

"You don't have kids, do you, Gloria?"

"I have done a heap of dumb things in my life, Frenchy, but that is not one of them. Why, are you afraid I'm going to spring some little surprise like that on you?"

"Hey, how long, I mean, I spent less than a week in New York with you, and I just got off the plane this afternoon. You might have a bunch of secrets."

"I don't, though, not from you. I showed you all my secrets again after dinner, didn't I?"

Frenchy, gratified that her love-making had roused Gloria to such heights, pulled her close. "You sure —"

"This isn't New York City, Frenchy!" protested Gloria. "We have to be careful in Vegas."

"What, there are no gay people here?"

"Look at this crowd!"

She turned her back on the amazing course of waterways that the builders of the Mirage Hotel had constructed in the middle of the desert and looked at the hundreds of paired women and men thronging the sidewalks, some of the younger ones herding their broods. "You're right. Straight and narrow. Where are the queers?"

"They have their own bars and casinos. We can go over to Paradise Road if you want, but I had other things in mind for us." She led Frenchy farther along the strip.

"I don't know if I can go a week without gay people," Frenchy worried. At home in the Village she was either at work or visiting people with AIDS or working with the neighborhood preservation group or hanging out at the bar on the corner. "Not everyone in my life is gay, but I'd have to estimate a good fifty percent are," she boasted.

"Aren't I gay enough?"

Frenchy grinned, remembering Gloria, pins out of her thick dark hair, breasts like globes waiting to be traveled, a white sheet just covering her hips, more inviting than sheer nakedness. She'd left the sheet there, sat on the bed, touching and touching, kissing and kissing everything above it until, with a little yip, Gloria had pulled her down and dislodged it herself.

"Yeah, you're gay enough," conceded Frenchy.

"Well then."

"It's hard to imagine, that's all. I never knew anybody like you. I mean, whoever thought Frenchy Tonneau, the original New York dyke, would get flown all the way out here by a woman fourteen years younger than her and richer than Donald Trump!"

"Are you really fifty, Frenchy?"

"Just turned fifty last month."

"You look, maybe, thirty-nine."

"I inherited young hair."

"Black as night."

"I'm surprised you Westerners know what night is."

"East Texas isn't like this, honey. Texas is a real place. Too real, sometimes," she said with a little sigh. "That's why this woman's got to leave it now and then if she wants to have a love life."

Frenchy stopped and a crowd of raucous teenagers carrying drinks swarmed around and passed them. "You mean I'm not the first woman you're meeting in Las Vegas?"

Gloria, about two inches taller, leaned to meet her eyes. Frenchy could see her cleavage where the cape parted, just above a gold-colored cocktail dress which shimmered in the blinking neon. "Honey," said Gloria, "practice makes perfect."

Though she'd strutted through her own string of girls when she was younger, before the nine years with Mercedes, she'd sworn off that kind of life. Gloria was the first woman she'd been slightly interested in for a long time and she'd accepted her persistent offer half-hoping to lure her back to the city. She'd pictured herself strolling the Village streets with this rich, beautiful, drawling woman on her arm.

Instead she felt like an exciting new toy Gloria could watch as she played tour guide.

Then again, she thought as that dress shimmered before her, Gloria hadn't exactly promised a trip to one of the neon-lit marriage chapels. Maybe being a toy would do for a few days.

Frenchy raised her left eyebrow and nodded in agreement, tongue in cheek. "Practice makes perfect."

"Well then," said Gloria, kittenish.

They stepped onto a covered, moving ramp. It carried them past reconstructions of scenes from ancient Rome. Through a window she saw real costumed couples strolling the paths of Caesar's Palace between columns lit in white. The enormous building was covered with thousands of red and yellow lights which gave the impression of gold. It occurred to her that Gloria had chosen her gold dress to match Caesar's Palace. What a woman.

No one else was in the passageway with them. Gloria took her hand. "That suit makes you even more appealing."

Frenchy stretched to her full 4'11", filled her chest with air and thrust her chin up. One of her friends was a costume-maker. When she'd mentioned this trip Amaretto had beamed with delight for her and asked, "What will you wear?" It had cost her, but Amaretto designed and sewed two tuxedos, one black with lavender trim, one white with violet. "It was like making doll clothes!" Amaretto said when she presented them to Frenchy. They had a fashion show right at the bar, with her changing in the bathroom and parading out for the whole neighborhood to cheer. She knew she looked good.

She shrugged at Gloria's praise as if she were used to wearing such finery, but she dropped her hand as they approached the mouth of the casino. They were disgorged into the most amazing space she'd ever seen. "Is this for real?"

Gloria laughed. "That's a matter of opinion."

Frenchy felt like a tourist in New York City. It was an effort to keep her mouth closed. There was so much to pay attention to. The famous singing group on a small stage in the middle of everything. The chandeliers and long mirrored bars. The green felt tables. The arcade-like signs reporting scores. The banks of TVs. The lavishly designed betting parlors. The slot machines — everywhere slot machines. The only thing there was more of was people.

"It's like Times Square, only these people have money," she said. Women in evening gowns sat playing the machines, three at a time, dropping coins in, cranking the arms of one, then the next, then the next. Now and then a machine burped back winnings.

"Wild enough for you, Frenchy?"

Wild, loud, confusing. "What do we do next?" When she was a kid she might have moved from table to bar to slot machine to table, but, although with Gloria she felt confident and smooth again, she knew she was no kid.

Gloria didn't blink at Frenchy's disorientation. "Come with me, honeybuns. Let's get some nickels and start you off big."

She didn't notice the time until after two AM when the pace at Caesar's Palace seemed to slacken a little. The merrymakers had departed; the diehard gamblers still worked. Frenchy had won seven hundred and fifty dollars, Amaretto's fee plus, by the time she cashed out at the window. Gloria had nineteen hundred. They took a cab to their hotel, a small place on a relatively quiet street just off the strip.

Gloria unhooked Frenchy's bow tie and made coffee. From their top floor window they could see the lights still blazing on a hotel that was a replica of a riverboat.

"It's hard to believe this is desert here. I mean," explained Frenchy, "like twenty-mule-team Borax and real mirages and all that."

"Mirages are never real," teased Gloria.

"That volcano was tonight."

"It was fire and water, but not a genuine volcano."

"I know. So even the real stuff is make believe."

"People who spend too long in Las Vegas can lose it. They don't know night from day. They can't make rational decisions about money. This is an upside-down town where sin is in, money is the end-all and be-all and everyone is forever young."

"How long is too long?"

"One night, for some folks, honey."

"I still know you're real."

"You'd better believe it," Gloria said, leaning over her on the couch and pressing Frenchy's head against that delicious cleavage.

Frenchy felt like the little girl hiding her face from the volcano.

They visited a different casino the next night, and the next.

"Don't you ever get tired of these things, Gloria?" she asked as they sat in an ornate restaurant. Half-naked women still precision-kicked through Frenchy's head to show music that still rang in her ears. Under Gloria's tutelage she'd increased her winnings to $1,200 which she'd converted to travelers' checks and stashed in the motel safe.

"I'll bet you think I'm a chronic party-girl," Gloria challenged.

"Well —"

"I can't blame you. You've only seen me traveling. And when I'm away from home I like to play a whole lot."

"I noticed."

"I need these vacations. Like I told you, sweet thing, it gets all *too* real back in Texas."

"What does?"

"Having Daddy's money. Making it grow so it won't go away. Giving it to the right causes without letting on that I'm helping to support that ol' militant homosexual agenda. You may think it's nice work if you can get it, but . . . it makes it hard to be me."

Gloria held out her cigarette to be lit. Frenchy had unearthed her old Zippo for the trip and used it with a flourish.

"That's why I go to strange cities to meet women," Gloria explained. "I'm looking for someone who wants me for me, not for my bank account. Money is a weight around my neck, something I can't escape. I just do not have the knack of living lightly. Look at you. I say dress casual and you wear a nice open-necked shirt and jeans. Me? A three-hundred-dollar jump suit in white that'll have to be thrown out if I get a drop of this sauce on it. I don't want to need all these things. I don't want to have all this power to change lives with Daddy's money. I hate my life, I hate me sometimes, and I don't know how to escape either."

The woman's seductive brown eyes were after more than a good time. Feverish, like the desert sun, would they melt or burn? She'd had enough experience to handle someone like Gloria, though. She polished the lighter on her thigh.

"I've been searching the whole world for the woman I want, Frenchy. She's got a permanent vacation lined up for her. We can travel and lounge, jump out of planes and dive under the sea. I can give her anything at all and I'll only attach one string: she's got to love me. I wouldn't think that'd be so hard."

Was Gloria trying to tell her something? She was about to ask when the waiter came with the dessert cart. She could almost feel her waist thicken as creamy chocolate melted on her tongue. When they stood to go she pulled her stomach in and looked at herself in one of the dozens of available mirrors. There, she was no menopausal has-been, she had the figure of a twenty-year-old still.

The next day they went to Death Valley in a rented car. Gloria drove far too fast. Frenchy was damned proud of how hard she worked and how important she was to her company. Just this once, though, she let herself dream in the air-conditioned, spanking new Mustang of a life of leisure, with this pretty brown-eyed lady entertaining her, giving her gifts, offering that greedy body up for more. She remembered her younger days, going along for the ride in another red convertible, on her first grown up vacation, to Provincetown. The young Frenchy had yearned for this good life then. Was it really within her grasp?

The roads out here so straight, the landscape up to the mountain ridges so unbroken. It was a bleak, hot, lifeless-looking place.

"I'll take the Lower East Side over this any day," she pronounced.

"We'll go up into some of the passes, honey. Then

you'll see splendor New York couldn't give you if the mayor hired an army of muralists."

Gloria pulled into Dante's View, over 5,000 feet up. Though still pretty boring, what with no buildings or parks or people, the sight was majestic. The sign said they were looking a mile down into the valley and twenty-one miles across to the next peak.

"I'll bet it was prettier when it was a lake."

"That was twelve thousand years ago, Frenchy. I can't impress you with anything, can I? Come on, let's have lunch."

The deli where they'd stopped on the way had packed them pastrami and swiss sandwiches on rye, with kosher dills and, the guy said, a special mustard imported from his uncle's shop in Hoboken.

"It's pretty strange sitting up here eating my usual lunch," commented Frenchy. "But it's a pretty good sandwich for Nevada." She liked to say the Western place names, they felt so foreign to her tongue. She liked to think of herself in an exotic setting with a beautiful woman on her arm.

The brown eyes pleaded with her. "Do you think you could ever live anyplace except New York?"

Was Gloria sounding her out? She was careful in her answer. "Not here."

They took a couple more day trips and had a marathon slot night when they both took $200 of their winnings and played quarter machines until they were tired.

"Geez Louise," said Frenchy at the end of it. "This must be play money, not the stuff I grub so hard for all week. I just lost it all and I'm laughing!"

Gloria laughed too, her face flushed. "It's a good

thing for you we agreed to split our winnings." She handed Frenchy $73.50. "Do you get tired of it? The grubbing?"

"Does rain get tired of falling? You just do it. I'm going to make manager at the store before I retire. They don't like lady managers, but I'll do it."

"That's so demeaning, having men tell you what you can or can't do."

"Where would you be except for your Daddy?"

Without a pause, brown eyes glowing, Gloria whispered, "Keeping house for a woman like you."

Frenchy narrowed her eyes and wished she still smoked. There were moments in life when cool was all-important. "Want to?"

"Leave Texas?"

"We could find a bigger apartment maybe. But mine is rent controlled and near the store."

Gloria pulled her into a bar and found a table for two. The bare-legged waitress stopped before they sat down.

"A bottle of your best champagne," Gloria ordered. She lowered her eyes at Frenchy's surprised look. "It's our last night and we're going to celebrate."

"Celebrate what?"

"I think I've found her."

Frenchy's heart pounded. Was Gloria really going to ask? Did she really want to wine her and dine her for the pleasure of her badass butch company? Maybe she'd cash in her pension and buy the red convertible she'd always dreamed of driving if she'd had a license, one of those small noisy sporty jobs. Hell, they could keep a pad in New York. She wouldn't be leaving forever.

The waitress served their champagne.

"Remember," Gloria asked, "when I talked about looking for the woman I could take home with me?"

"Kind of," Frenchy mumbled.

"I'm not all that fussy, Frenchy. I've actually tried a few women. I figure one week of shacking up someplace glamorous doesn't predict forever."

Her ego plunged. So she'd just be another in a long line of gold-diggers.

"But you. I want to celebrate being with you because you are the woman I never thought I'd find. It's in your every gesture, in everything you say. Usually I don't have to wait till the last night to find an opening, but you are so self-sufficient, so proud, you're the right stuff. I truly admire you, Frenchy Tonneau."

"For what?" she asked, still feigning innocence. Was there anything besides fire in Gloria's eyes? Affection? Regret?

"You're the only woman I've met who'd say no to me. I won't even insult you with the question. You're devoted to your career, your friends, your city. You're just the woman I'd want, but I wouldn't ruin you by stealing you away from your life." Gloria raised her glass. "To the woman who would refuse me."

Frenchy flushed. "Yeah," she said, feeling foolish, feeling like she'd been caught with her hand in the cookie jar, feeling unmasked even if only to herself.

Probably, she thought, *probably, I would have said no.*

She could see the mirage of that dream-life burn and disappear with a hiss, drowned in a pool of real life. She didn't want to look at Gloria, but there was nowhere to hide from those volcanic eyes.

TRUE LOVE
Fruitstand IV

Did you see that moon last night, Bookworm? Looked like a Sunkist billboard up there, a big painted fruit all orange and full. I wanted to peel it, see what it is about the moon that drives people nuts.

My guess is we're going to be busy as the dickens later. First off, the moon makes the customers hungry. If they can't have true love they want full bellies, am I right? The other reason, remember this

93

day last month? You college kids — your memory only goes back as far as your last meal.

Oh. Your last roll in the hay. Knowing you, that's not very long at all. How many girlfriends have you had so far this year — and you're only a freshman? You work harder at finding your true love than anyone I've ever met.

Anyway, it's food stamp day. And it's Saturday. The customers will start late, but when they come there won't be a lemon or a grape left on the shelf. I'll ring the register, you restock. And no dumping things in the bins please, Bookworm. Make the oranges look like full moons and the kiwi fruit like candy so they'll buy them for a treat. That's how you make a profit in this business, the extras, not the staples.

What about who? I don't remember who I was talking about yesterday afternoon. No, I'm not getting decrepid, I just have more important things on my mind. So give me a hint.

Kathy's cousin. The gay one. You're a great help. Do you know how many gay in-laws I've got? There's Adele and Irene and Mike and Mitzi and Steven here in Queens just for starters. If all Kathy's gay relatives were talking to one another they could rent every square inch of Cherry Grove for themselves and their lovers and ex-lovers and no one else would fit.

The pretty old lady who was cruising you by the overripe bananas last week? That's Mitzi. She lives over on Eighty-ninth Street. Nice elderly building, rent-controlled. She's been there forever. She worked till retirement in a hospital on Welfare Island, a licensed practical nurse with people who never got released. Almost never. This was a long time ago.

94

You have to be a certain kind of person to deal with that, with kids who wouldn't get any care at home even if they were 100 percent so they have to live in the hospital to stay alive. I always wondered what kind of life that is to stay alive for, but I guess if it was what I had I'd take it with thanks. Mitzi also had grownups too sick or hurt to care for themselves. And old people without a clue who they are any more and nobody wants to clean their diapers, but they haven't got the insurance for a nursing home. Which is just as well the way some of those homes are run, am I right?

Anyway, Mitzi is Kathy's mom's cousin, Kathy's second cousin. Yes, there are dykes even older than me, Bookworm. I'm only fifty-six.

She never hid what she is either. Kathy had Mitzi to run to the first time she fell for a slick little butch in boots and a ducktail haircut. Mitzi had one living with her at the time, as a matter of fact. Mitzi's butch was there one day when Kathy was visiting and about knocked Kathy's socks off. It was the style then, you know, cool as ice, never a smile, but eyes that promised the Garden of Eden if you'd just give her a dance.

No, I wasn't ever like that. Kathy had some sense knocked into her by the time she got to me. She wanted a solid woman who wouldn't skip out on her when the going got tough. And I haven't; we celebrate our thirtieth anniversary pretty soon. Right, it is awesome.

But Mitzi taught Kathy the ropes, femme to femme, you know, and was there for Kathy to brag about her lovers, or after break-ups, or in between girlfriends. She must have been fifty or so when

Kathy and me got together. I remember Kathy dragged me over to Eighty-ninth Street to meet Mitzi and I polished my boots till you could see your face in them. I knew I was getting inspected and I wanted that stamp of approval like I never wanted anything before in my life. Except Kathy.

Of course Mitzi looks like an old lady. What do you think, femmes are exempt from wrinkles? Well, yeah, she is exempt from gray hair. She never had money, but she knew how to use the riches she was born with. That auburn hair comes down to her calves, which isn't all that long considering how pint-sized she is.

We visit her now and then, and Mitzi makes sure she sits at Kathy's station at the diner every morning for breakfast.

What do you mean is that all she did with her life: nursing, seducing butches and combing her hair? What are you doing with your life except breaking hearts? You're eighteen and you have no plans? Anthropology? What kind of work is that, going around collecting stories like Mitzi's. You should be a doctor or a teacher, help somebody. What good will it do to write books about old femmes?

For your information, though, Mitzi did make a difference. It was hard work she did at the hospital. She'd go in every holiday to make the days special. And why not? Her girlfriends always had family they had to be with and of course they couldn't bring a gay lover home to Mom. So Mitzi stayed all day with her patients and if there was time, spent the evening with her family. She *still* goes to the hospital with presents even now. She loves those people.

Maybe more than was good for her.

Kathy told me all about Mitzi-the-femme: life of the party, dancing till dawn, the siren of Greenwich Village. Even when she was a kid she hated her plain-jane name, Miriam, and pestered the family to call her after vampy Great Aunt Mitzi. She got a ring from every lover she was with and wears them, all at the same time, to this day. The men were always after her, but she was a woman's woman, am I right? She was looking for her true love.

Darn, where are all the customers? We should have had a few early birds at least. Maybe the mail was late; people will have a hard time making it till Monday if it was. Yeah, I give a little bit of credit, but it's not such a hot idea. When they get the stamps they buy stuff they need even more and don't have anything left for old bills. So I have to wait for the welfare to come. But the old people save me. They get their pensions earlier and they always pay cash. I scold them for carrying it all around on them. They don't want to pay the bank fees so what else can they do except risk the muggers? It must be hard getting used to the world turning out so rotten, like watching a kid grow into a criminal.

Right, we were talking about Mitzi. All of a sudden she stopped going out. Now this is before I knew Kathy, before I even knew I was gay, so I'm getting it secondhand. Ancient history. The stuff you won't find in books.

You're going to write books about Mitzi — and me? All right, all right, you are. Maybe I should start calling you Dreamer. I definitely won't switch to Dreamboat, though. What do the girls see in you?

You're going to be famous? Who ever heard of a famous archeologist. Anthropologist then. Margaret Mead? Never heard of her. Is she gay?

So Mitzi drops out of sight nights. She catches the subway every morning, but she comes home at all hours, still in uniform. Finally Kathy's mom goes to see her, but Mitzi's not talking. So Kathy's mom grabs Steven, figuring one of the gay cousins might get more out of her. He strikes out. It's Adele, who's only sixteen at the time, but has been with her true love two years by then, who finally gets through.

Adele goes alone after school to the hospital. When she gets home, Peppie — you know her, she's the one who runs numbers over at the cigar store — thinks Adele's seen a ghost she's so white. Kathy got the whole story from Peppie.

It seems like Mitzi is seeing someone at the hospital. Not staff either. I mean, she couldn't find some lady doctor and set herself up good, could she? No, she falls for a patient. A paralyzed, terminal patient. Why do people get themselves into situations that can only end, can you answer me that with your college education?

What doesn't end? Good answer, Bookworm. You think it's easier knowing the end like Mitzi thought she did than making believe it won't come? No? Then what? Maybe you're right: human beings love hope. So tell me, is true love the one that lasts, or is it the one where your hopes go as high as the moon?

Bett was Mitzi's age exactly and from the pictures Peppie showed us, a good-looking woman. Way too thin, of course, and tense, like someone who needs to be angry but hasn't got the energy. Still, that old butchy magic hadn't disappeared. Mitzi combed her hair back for her and Bett posed with the cigarette Mitzi put in her mouth, like Bogart. Bett would squint over it and could blow smoke rings out of one corner of her mouth at the same time as she held the cigarette in the other side.

How'd she get that way? Hit-and-run accident. She was the only woman in the garment district hauling clothes, not sewing. You know how the guys do it, dashing across streets, walking with the traffic, pushing those racks on wheels. Count your blessings that we don't have to peddle fruit along Roosevelt Avenue like my father did when he started out. My insurance would go higher than even your hopes.

Well, one day Bett was out there crossing the street with an empty and this car comes screeching around the corner and brakes, but way too late. Bett's down, her spine hurt real bad, and a knock on the head from the fall. The driver backs up, pulls around her and takes off. Nobody got the license, nothing. Also, from the bang on the head, Bett's out cold for months. She doesn't carry i.d., no driver's license, nothing.

See, she was passing. You know, pretending she was a guy so she could get work that didn't pin her down to a sewing machine or a typewriter. She took the job because she was paid under the table, no questions asked.

So no one comes looking for her. And when she comes out of it about all she can remember is her first name — at least they thought it was her first name. They called her Betty. A couple of months later the whole name came back to her, Bettina Sola, but the hospital social worker couldn't find relatives.

Meanwhile, the cops talked to people at her job —

thinking it might not have been an accident. Everybody said she'd played it real close, like she had something to hide. Then this one guy said he'd seen her — him, he'd thought — going in and out of a building in his neighborhood in the East Village. It wasn't exactly trendy down there then. The landlord told the cops that Bett shared a one room cold-water walk up with another woman and they took off without paying the rent. "The pretty one probably went home to Missouri where she should have stayed in the first place, away from these deviants," the cops quoted him in a report.

Meanwhile Bett was getting back bits and pieces of her past. Like when summer came, the calendar showed woods. A couple of weeks staring at that and she remembered growing up in the Bronx, near Pelham Bay Park. Missouri triggered something else. She remembered the woman she'd lived with, but there was no way she could even start to find her.

Legs and arms dead, the only blessing of the accident was that she could talk, and after a while read if someone turned the pages for her. A lot of good it did her to talk, though. She was scared to death to tell anyone that she and Missouri had been lovers.

They'd been together a year and a half, had enough high hopes to beat the band, were saving money to look for work down in Jersey, somewhere in the country. Bett thought she could get a job as a house painter, though she couldn't now remember why. Missouri would be a store clerk, like she'd been back home. They just needed a car and then they could start looking for an old farmhouse to rent.

They'd planned to stay together forever, but after the accident, Bett figured, Missouri must have thought she'd taken off on her. Bett also thought it was just as well. She wasn't supposed to live long, something about complications in that kind of injury. I never understood it, Bookworm, just felt for the gal.

The pits is right. It could happen to anyone, but when it happens to one of us, especially when it's a man who turns out to be a woman, and there's no such thing as a marriage record, and no blood relatives who care enough to go looking, well, there's nothing they can do but pop her in a place like Mitzi's hospital.

She got there about a year after the accident. Before that there were times she couldn't even breathe on her own. They were afraid to give her therapy because of risks. Mitzi got all the hardest cases. While she rested up from her transfer Bett just lay there like a vegetable getting turned every couple of hours.

One day in the spring Mitzi went to change her sheets and Bett smiled at her for the first time. Mitzi told Adele she almost keeled over from the power of it. Like walking into a room and there's the full moon grinning at her.

Afterwards, Mitzi claimed she already knew. They wheel in this middle-aged woman with short curly hair, no trace of family and worldly goods consisting of a comb, a pack of cigarettes and one of those old Browni radios, the Cadillac of transistors. Plus she gets this faraway look in her eyes when a Timi Yuro song comes on.

Mitzi just couldn't be sure. You take a perfectly

good butch type and throw a hospital nightgown on her, take away her swagger and her hand talk and how's anyone supposed to know who's in that bed?

Until she smiled. Mitzi said it hit her right in the you-know-what, down there. Don't use that word! It's dirty, that's why. I don't care if the Queen of England is *reclaiming* it. Which I doubt. It doesn't belong in a palace anymore than a shop. Shh. The customers might hear you.

Mitzi jumped to attention when she saw that smile. The Browni was singing a love song in the background. Then Bett gave her the look. I'll bet even you can't seduce a woman with nothing but your eyes and a smile.

First Mitzi started spending her breaks with Bett, then her lunch hours. She'd always given her all to any patient, but it'd been professional; she knew better than to give her heart away to people who couldn't stop themselves from leaving her.

After a while she started cooking dinner at home the night before and heating it up at the hospital to eat with Bett. Then Mitzi started going over there on her days off, staying after her shifts, arriving early. When true love came, it hit hard.

Outside she'd been seeing this woman known all over the bars for her jealousy. The woman stormed the hospital. "You're not breaking another date with me or I'm breaking somebody's leg."

She'd found Mitzi reading *The Girls In Three B* aloud to Bett. The jealous lover wasn't dumb.

"You don't play fair, Mitz. How can I break *her* leg?" She glared at the two of them. I don't know who was more helpless, the woman or Bett, cool as a cuke with her hand in Mitzi's. "You just better keep this quiet, bitch. I don't want any of my friends wondering what she's got that I don't."

The hospital staff didn't seem to mind. Mitzi had made sure that they knew about her being gay already, and, well, whatever comfort another human being could give Bett, more power to her was the attitude. Wouldn't it be nice if the whole world thought like that? It's a hard life, Bookworm, as you'll find out, college education or no, and why people want to deprive themselves and others of some loving words and tender touches I'll never know.

Whoa, a customer! There's Mrs. Marseglia. She's good for seven apples, some garlic and two pounds of greens anyway. Mrs. Marseglia! Come on in before the crowds pick it all over! What? Maybe it'll come in today's mail then. You bet, I'll see you later, no rush. If you haven't gotten yours no one has.

What did I tell you, Bookworm? It's the mail. Or the government. I suppose you'd have me move my business into Forest Hills where people live on cash, not stamps. Don't you forget your roots, with all this education. Don't you forget your own kind here under the elevated hawking apples or caring for the bedridden.

Did they make love? It was all making love, Bookworm. Mitzi made love to Bett every time she spent an extra minute at her side. Bett made love to Mitzi with her words, her eyes, the songs on her radio. Adele visited sometimes and she told Peppie she'd never seen anything like it. Mitzi would caress Bett's cheek and Adele swore Bett's lashes could flutter like Cupid's wings. Or Mitzi would take her hand and Bett's eyes would stroke Mitzi's breasts. Of course Bett could kiss too, though they never did that in front of Adele.

And Mitzi! She had to wear her uniform at work, but she festooned herself till she looked, Peppie said, like an Easter bonnet. Flowers, perfumes, glittery pins, makeup to beat the band and of course her hair, her long flowing glowing hair tied up with ribbons or bright barrettes. She'd take Bett's limp hand and stroke her own hair with it by the hour. Bett told her she could feel it, but no one really knew. I guess it didn't matter. It was making love, am I right?

If I couldn't love Kathy the way I'm used to, I'd do it any way I could, too. But I'd want the same things with her that I have right now. Living together for instance. Mitzi and Bett were just like anyone else. After they'd been going together several months, Mitzi wanted to bring Bett home. I know, I know. Bett needed constant care, but they wanted to be alone together too, not stuck on a ward with a bunch of other people. Mitzi did get her moved into a room with only four beds, but at least one of the others was always occupied. Bett longed to be in an apartment, with her bed up to the window, raised so she could look out at birds, or the street. And Mitzi wanted to spend some time at home again; she was always at the hospital.

Mitzi's cousins and a couple of friends, one who was a nurse, volunteered time so Bett could be home while Mitzi was at work. They were very excited, just a step away from their big dream. Mitzi went to the hospital administrator.

"I heard you were dedicated," the gruff man told

her, "but don't you think you're going too far?" She couldn't persuade him that she wasn't overworked to the point of obsession, or trying to do a patient out of an inheritance.

When she didn't let up, Mr. Gruff looked into it some more and smelled something queer. Very queer.

"Keep this up and you'll lose your job," he threatened her. "We can't have this kind of thing going on here. We have the hospital's reputation to uphold. If the public gets wind that you've been corrupting the patients — we'll have no choice but to let you go. Now stay away from the Sola woman or you'll be on the unemployment line."

The idea of staying away from her lover was as stupid to Mitzi as the idea of selling raspberries from a bin of tomatoes is to me. Mr. Gruff might not know she was the top L.P.N. in the city, but her supervisors knew to protect her. They looked away when she was with Bett.

Then it occurred to Mitzi that if she were related to Bett, no one could stop them from doing whatever they decided. She tried to find a way to marry her, but couldn't do it legally — though what harm they think it'd do for us to have rights like the next person I don't know.

Somebody made a joke about adopting Bett. Mitzi thought she'd never heard a better idea. They allow that nowadays, but back then, when they investigated, Mitzi's brazen past came up and they dropped her application like she was out to murder Bett, not love her.

By this time Mitzi's tired, damn tired. She's still totally in love with this woman who would charm her with compliments and tales of her sexy past. Mitzi said she'd never felt so appreciated in all her life. But she wanted to come home to Bett at night, not sneak in to see her at odd moments and leave at the end of visiting hours, which the supervisors insisted on after Mr. Gruff laid down the law.

Her next scheme had to do with finding someone in Bett's family. The authorities considered Bett incompetent ever since the coma. All Mitzi needed was one blood relative with a sympathetic ear to sign her out and then Mitzi would take over. Was that too much to ask? Bett was no help. Whole parts of her life were missing, like what schools she'd gone to, who'd been her friends as a kid.

Mitzi followed the earlier path the police had taken and came to the same dead end. There was only one other avenue she could try: Missouri. If Bett was such a storyteller now, talking and talking until her memory stopped her, maybe she'd been that way with Missouri, and maybe Missouri would remember something. Could be she'd even kept Bett's stuff.

But almost two years after the accident, Bett couldn't remember Missouri's name.

Adele went with Mitzi to the landlord. He didn't want to cooperate with them any more than he had with the social worker, but Mitzi was desperate. Adele said Mitzi flirted and pleaded and wouldn't give up. Finally, the landlord scribbled something on a piece of paper. Adele said Mitzi's hands were shaking as she looked, outside on the crowded sidewalk, at the information. "Leah Seals," she read. "One-twenty-one Oak Street, Baring, Missouri. We've got hope again!"

These days I suppose you'd call the woman and get

it over with. Back then long distance was still a kind of expensive magic to my family, so Mitzi went home and wrote her a letter on hospital paper she'd "borrowed" just for that. Adele helped her compose it. It was the bare bones, not a word about love. Mitzi went to the hospital and read it to Bett. Then she crossed her fingers.

She crossed Bett's fingers too. This was their last resort.

Over a week went by. Mitzi had asked Leah Seals to write directly to Bett. Every morning when the patient mail was delivered Mitzi went through it before the Candy Striper could distribute it. On the tenth day, still nothing. On the eleventh day, a Sunday, they could only wait for Monday.

Or so they thought.

Visiting hours had just ended and Mitzi was getting away with staying a little later since staff was low on Sunday nights. They heard a commotion at the other end of the hall. "Must be one of the kids acting up," Bett said with a laugh. Then they heard a voice just outside Bett's door.

"I've come all the way from Missouri! You better let go of me."

The nurse on duty rushed into the doorway, trying to block the way. She looked over her shoulder at Mitzi with horrified eyes.

"Bett!" cried Leah Seals. "Oh, Bett, Bett, Bett! Why didn't you tell me? I thought you'd walked out on me!"

The nurse and Mitzi were holding Leah Seals back.

"You could kill her!" they were yelling. "She can't be barged into!"

Leah stood still, chest heaving, eyes pouring tears. Bett looked from Leah to Mitzi as if they both were trying to kill her.

"I'll be careful," promised Leah.

She was a slender woman, with pale skin and a wrinkled dress under a cardigan. She put a worn canvas bag on the floor and moved toward Bett, pushing nondescript hair from her eyes. Mitzi could tell that fixed up she'd be very pretty.

"My heart has been broken for two years," she told Bett. "I went home and moved back in with Mom. I just didn't have the spirit for cities anymore, or for love. Tell me what happened." She turned to Mitzi. "Tell me what I can do. Can I kiss her? Can she talk?"

Mitzi, still in uniform, moved backwards toward the door. She couldn't say a word. It hadn't ever occurred to her that Leah would want Bett again, like this, after all this time. Bett watched Mitzi with her eyes pleading. But for what, Mitzi wondered. For Mitzi to understand that Bett would have to go with Leah now? Mitzi left.

Oh! Mrs. Suarez! I'm sorry. We were talking and didn't notice you were ready. Did the mail come? I guess so. What can we do for you?

Yes, beautiful mangoes this week. They'll cost you out of season like this, but I grabbed them. I know my customers. You want the full ten pounds of oranges? I'll put them right in your shopping wagon. And there's your neighbor, Mrs. Avilla, and Mrs. Kho.

Look sharp, Bookworm. The day has begun. The end of the story? Quick, before they get to the register, come here.

Leah had brought a letter from her mother, using who knows what threats, saying Leah was Bett's sister. Don't ask me why Mr. Gruff took their word for it, maybe to end a bad situation for the hospital. At least Leah wasn't a staff member. Bett decided to leave.

Why? Because she couldn't choose between them. She told one of the other nurses that she hoped the trip would kill her because she didn't want to decide. Remember, the doctors said complications could do her in. They wanted her to stay put. It wasn't, the note she dictated said, that she didn't want to be with Mitzi, but she hated being a burden on anyone and the end would be quicker this way.

By the middle of the next week Leah had taken Bett's radio, cigarettes and smile to Missouri. Mitzi hoped Leah would at least let her know when Bett died, but lo and behold, the first letter was from Bett herself. She'd dictated it to Leah's mother.

The doctors had been wrong. She'd been moved plenty, she said, and she wasn't dead yet. She missed Mitzi, but things were easier in the country and Mrs. Seals took care of her while Leah was at work. Mitzi could have a real lover now, like she deserved. She'd made all those forever promises to Leah when they'd been together and she thought she ought to keep them.

Baring, Missouri, she said, was like a little heaven. Now that they knew it was safe, she could sit in a wheelchair out on Mom's porch. Leah clerked at the general store, then came home and cooked pies and huge country meals for her. She was getting fat watching the hummingbirds drink pink stuff and listening to the robins serenade the world.

THE WET NIGHT
At A Bar XIV

    Sometimes, especially in spring, when Sally the bartender goes from Cafe Femmes into the tart mid evening air, she is filled with wanderlust. Tired, she'll meander home for what seems like hours through the perhaps wet streets of the city, hardly aware that her black felt crusher has begun to smell like damp wool and to drip as she pauses at corners, where she sways enchanted by the sharp reflection of red traffic lights in puddles, or by the sight of bright moist

111

rows of strawberries, oranges, bananas and apples gleaming under the neon signs of small Korean-owned groceries.

Most of the time, she feels full with this feast. Now and then, though, she aches for Liz to be by her side.

Blonde Sally opens Cafe Femmes in the morning. Shorter, dark-haired Liz closes it at night. They spend their day off together and sleep every night touching through the dawn hours, forcing themselves awake to talk a few minutes as Liz comes to bed or Sally gets up. This schedule makes their time together delicious, even after all these years.

Tonight, Sally is drawn to a certain brownstone off West Fourth Street, as she would be to a secret lover. The owners of the building have preserved lilac bushes on tiny plots of ground to either side of its steps. During her worst fits of springtime roving their phosphorescent glow lures Sally, especially in the rain, to a scent that bursts like a billion lavender explosions. She breathes them and breathes them until she is dizzy with oxygen and reels off into the night, longing to make love.

It's then that every woman on the street turns into a siren, and then that Sally walks among them like a connoisseur in a statue garden, drinking in every line.

That one with the wide splash of lipstick, blowzy, on the rakish man's arm. She wears an old-fashioned wide-brimmed hat, has hips Sally could spend a whole night kissing her way across. The woman's perfume rivals the lilacs for loudness, even makes Sally sneeze, but she stares after the couple, knowing the woman will laugh a full pleased laugh as they begin, later, in a creaking rented bed.

She loved that Liz laughs in bed, respectful of their lovemaking, but not serious.

She turns onto Sixth Avenue, where there are more people, and her heart lurches after a quick-stepping fashion plate. Sally names her Nicole. Out of the Balducci's shopping bag on Nicole's arm peeps a baguette. She looks like she would not laugh during sex, and would allow into her life only lovers who did not disrupt her agenda. She would use the word *agenda*. Even now she scurries to prepare a pretty, perfect platter for a midnight dinner: parsley just so, bread rounds toasted an exact tan, the apricot wine chosen for its color against her delicately patterned crystal. Nicole believes it's healthy to come once a day, hasn't the time to bother with more. Sally wants to stroke that prim sharp nose, pry the thin lips apart and find the lush tongue with her own. Wants just once to tear innumerable abandoned climaxes from the woman which would leave them both sobbing and laughing and glad.

She passes a bar with an awning and considers returning to Cafe Femmes, where she could shadow Liz, spread her fingers across her bottom at opportune moments, steal kisses from a mouth sweet with the peppermints Liz uses to quell the taste of smoke.

The thought takes her back to the night, a month ago, when she'd woken from a seamy dream seething with desire. In it, a woman had been above her, open legs straddling Sally's face, pressing herself gently but rhythmically against Sally's pursed sticky lips and drumming tongue. Awake, her eyes still closed, Sally had exhaled a long breath. Her hand had discovered that Liz was home, sitting up in bed. She'd been reading *The Sunday Times*. Not a promising sign.

"Hi, babe," said Sally, hoping Liz would recognize in that endearment Sally's state. She was rubbing Liz's thigh with a finger.

"You're tickling," Liz said, squirming.

Sally turned onto her stomach. Her legs became entangled in the lower sheets.

"You're stealing the covers again, long tall Sal," said Liz, tugging them back across her lap.

Sally reached an arm across Liz's hips, accidentally on purpose disturbing the newspaper.

"Sal!"

Finally, Liz gave her a sideways glance. Her eyes narrowed at the sight of the big wide-eyed grin Sally had prepared.

"Uh-oh," said Liz. "You're up to no good."

"You sure about that?" Sally asked, pressing herself against Liz's leg and rubbing avidly.

Liz had laughed then, filling the air with the smell of peppermint toothpaste. It had been a laugh so like that of the blowsy woman with the wide-brimmed hat and loud perfume that Sally's mind returns to Sixth Avenue now. She realizes that she's walked uptown two blocks without seeing a thing. The rain has stopped.

She wants more this night than going home and waiting for Liz. She turns east on Eighth Street where the weekend crowds are teeming and she joins their restless hunt for pleasure.

Sally wanders toward the sound of a woman singing. She is white and middle-aged, a long-haired street musician in peasant clothing, back-lit by an open book shop. Two light-skinned adolescent boys accompany her, one with short elegantly waved black hair and a fiddle, the other with a wild reddish Afro and a banjo. An antique hippie and her sons? The woman's long skirt sways as she sings, brushing the tops of bare feet. Over an embroidered blouse she wears a fringed leather vest dyed purple; her breasts push against it. Sally smells the spicy patchouli and is overwhelmed by the strength of it as she imagines her head between those breasts. She tosses money in the hat for the delight of looking.

"Any requests?" asks the singer.

Sally sorts through her skimpy knowledge of folk music. " 'Mr. Tamborine Man?' " she asks, afraid the song had been too popular for a real folkie to deign to sing. But the woman, who has no Baez voice, but rather a full-throated, almost bluesy style, throws herself into it as if this is her all-time favorite tune. Sally taps her feet and realizes how much she'd wanted to hear such a pied-piper song tonight.

Once, when they'd still been new, just before they'd closed the deal on the bar, Liz had rented a car and they'd driven out of the city, without a destination, playing "Mr. Tamborine Man" and "Just Like A Woman" and "Lay Lady Lay" all the way to the end of Long Island, to Orient Point, where they'd waved goodbye to a ferryload of people who were crossing to Connecticut. As much as she'd cherished the thought of marriage to Liz — and buying that bar had been their marriage oath — she'd felt as if the Mr. Tamborine man in herself had been on that ferry. She smiles now, aware that he never left. She edges out of the crowd which swells around the singer. "Mr. Tamborine Man" follows Sally up the street.

It's about 9:30, long past dinner. At a deli she buys a package of apricot fruit leather in honor of the prim fashion plate and her pretty wine. She gnaws on the sour sheet of it until it seems sweet in her mouth. At Fifth Avenue, cloyed with the taste, she turns uptown to feed her other hungers.

A pack of punk girls who can't be over fifteen move toward her. Their hair ranges from pink to light green, some of it spiked, some crewcut, some cut stark and straight-edged. Like a cotton-candy chorus line, they jangle their jewelry and pop their gum and walk to the rhythm of a raucous oversized tape player. Underneath the racoon eyes, though, Sally sees the same tender flesh she'd first kissed, and loved, at their age. Behind the heavy odor of pot, she knows there is still the fresh scent only young girls have, when their pores exhale dreams and sex is still a new kind of play. Her body recalls the heaviness of her own young need, knows her underpants will be damp the rest of the way home tonight, as they always were back then.

There is one teenager, at the very end of the cotton candy line, who meets her eyes. She's at least partly Asian, wears jeans, and her hair is not as loud as the others'. The dyke, Sally thinks. She feels the girl's curiosity burn into her, feels the girl's desire to take what Sally knows and learn it for herself, the where-do-I-put-my-hand-and-when, and my tongue? Really, my tongue? And will you show me? Will you do it to me? Can I do it to you? Again? And again, please? Sally shivers at the thought of that slight frame, that new mouth on — not hers, but another fifteen-year-old who thinks she will die from the excitement.

Her legs feel tired. The fruit leather has been her only dinner. At the next corner she walks quickly back over to Sixth and signals a taxi. The driver is a heavy black woman who slouches against the side of the cab, one hand on the wheel, driving with a casualness Sally admires. She can see the woman's profile and wonders about her. Can someone so in control of her vehicle be anything but a lesbian? She wishes the bullet proof barrier between them were open, so she could make small talk, probe with gay hints. Would the woman think she was trying to pick her up? If she did, would Sally follow through?

What would it be like, a one-night, a one-hour stand with a stranger? Sally had never done that. Would they go up to Sally's? Would the driver know a secret nook near the docks? Would she get in back with Sally? Would she take off Sally's wet jacket, then open her shirt? It was unthinkable that Sally could be the aggressor with this authoritative woman.

The driver, leaning against a door, would pull Sally's back to spongy breasts, would cradle her, talk to her in a strange baritone. She'd snake her hands around and maneuver Sally's pants down to her calves, push Sally's legs apart in order to explore her with those wide strong hands, twist Sally's head around to kiss her with a bold tongue, with a mouth that smelled of cigarettes. Sally would press against the driver's hand, her breath short, her desire for release desperate beyond any craving she normally had. She'd push against the heel of that hand with her clitoris while the fingers played around her opening. Self-conscious, she'd strain and strain. The driver, making wet sounds against her ear, would try to make her come despite the awkwardness of the back seat, despite Sally's feeling of helplessness at being so exposed, at being so passive. She'd expect to come suddenly, powerfully, at the thought of her unaccustomed passivity, abandoning her inhibitions to the majesty of the woman. But she wouldn't, too discomfited by strangeness. Finally, she'd lie weak against the driver, not knowing if she should apologize or just reciprocate. The muffled traffic sounds, the sight of dark warehouses, the fact of Liz, would seep back into her consciousness. She'd turn around on the woman's breasts, really look at her for the first time, not just a hand, and not Liz, but another real person, a stranger.

And then? Then the woman would repulse Sally's advances, mutter about not wanting to get done, drive her home and refuse a tip. Sally would be left standing on the curb, still admiring the big woman with the deft hands and the air of command.

They'd reached the theater district. Sally rapped on the window to get out, half-afraid she'd revealed her thoughts in some way, perhaps through the fantasy meter ticking away on the dashboard. Embarrassed by the feeling of intimacy she had for this stranger, she tipped her too much. Sally stepped outside the cab and turned to the driver with a sheepish smile. Without a glance at her, the driver zoomed to the mouth of a theater and picked up a woman and a man. Sally felt empty, abandoned, yet exhilarated. She'd had the pleasure of the encounter without the complication of reality. Liz need never know anything but Sally's spillover of passion.

Marquees blinked and blazed above her. She stood

watching as the theaters emptied and the streets filled. Then the rain came down again. She wanted to laugh, to raise her mouth to the sky and catch the plummeting raindrops. A woman squealed. A man held a huge black umbrella straight out, chest-level, and opened it mechanically with a whoosh. Now the umbrellas blossomed all up and down Broadway, slick and jouncing. Sally leapt over puddles in a private ballet, jubilant at having joined this huge party.

A lone woman in her sixties passed her in a belted trench coat and a rain hat slanted down over her eyes. All Sally could see of her face was a finely drawn mouth in faint lipstick under a long nose. The woman walked swiftly in sturdy black high heels, her hands in her slash pockets. Sally waited a while, then set off after her.

The rain muffled all sounds. The woman maneuvered through the crowds. She called no cab, but moved up Broadway with purpose. They passed restaurants and a few small markets. Sally's stomach grumbled, her hat dripped, her feet were sore and wet inside their running shoes, but the magnet of this woman, who was probably sixty-five or seventy, drew her past crosstown streets that were more devoid of traffic with every uptown block. Their only company was a parking garage attendant who stood in a gaping entranceway, arms folded, watching them go by. Sally nodded back at him.

She would tell Liz about this woman later. About the Amazon who stalked Broadway, luring younger women through the dangerous city.

Where would they end up if the Amazon had her way with Sally? On the very private balcony of a high-rise on Fifth Avenue, she decided. They would drink coffee the next morning in the Sunday sunlight. Young couples would stroll far beneath them with baby carriages. Roller skaters, joggers, looking very small, would enter the park. Widowers would snooze on the benches that line Fifth Avenue, and women would chatter to one another across them.

The woman in the trench coat would recline on a chaise lounge, her hair gray-white, her cheeks lined graphs around the jutting nose. Sally would reach to the woman's long robe and slide it open, letting her fingers rest on the gray hair between her legs. Their eyes would meet. The woman's lips, newly colored, would part. She'd let her legs fall open just enough. Sally would push into the still-damp nest from a shower they'd shared and her finger, barely touching, would roll back and forth, back and forth on the woman's stiff clitoris until her orgasm came, like another ray of warm sunlight, as quiet as the rain-washed Sunday city and the swarming park so far below.

But the woman in the trench coat didn't turn east on Fifty-ninth. Instead, she crossed as if going into the park. Sally drew the line there. She did not go into Central Park at night. She wanted to stop the woman, warn her, a hovering lover.

But she wasn't. The woman veered west, away from the park, and Sally watched her enter the Plaza Hotel. Sally walked past the doors, craning her neck. An out-of-towner, she thought. Of course.

She was near home now. It was almost midnight and she knew Spot needed her walk, so she plunged through the rain the last few blocks, grabbed the Sunday papers and an hour later was in bed where she slept soundly until three A.M.

"Sal?"

Sally tried to wake up.

"I'm home, Sal," whispered Liz, and Sally at long last felt a naked woman's body covering her own.

She could smell city rain mixed with bar smoke on her lover's hair, and the peppermint toothpaste. Liz's skin felt tight from the night's tensions; her voice sounded a little raw from talking over the juke box. The windows were closed, but Sally could hear a squalling baby in the apartment across the courtyard. Liz's body met hers in all the important places, softness mixed with hard curves.

"Romantic, isn't it?" she asked.

"You mean the baby?" Liz laughed softly, rubbing her pubic hair against Sally's so it made the tiniest crinkly sound. Then she lay still against Sally with a sigh.

Sally feared that Liz would fall asleep. She ran her hands down the curves of Liz's back, rested her fingers around her waist, then began to stroke down Liz's bottom over and over, spreading the cheeks a tiny bit each time she reached the bottom.

"Umm," said Liz.

Sally reached lower so that her spreading would pull Liz's lips slightly apart. "Do you like that?" She couldn't quite reach inside.

"All of it, Sal. I kept feeling your hands on me all night. I don't know what set me off."

"Whatever it was, I'll take it."

Liz opened her legs, tucked her feet around Sally's knees. This brought her higher. Sally slipped one finger in.

"Hhhh," gasped Liz. She pushed down on Sally's finger.

"I'd say you're ready, baby. Want to roll over?"

Liz shook her head against Sally's neck.

Sally moved her finger in circles, around and around inside the wet fleshy tent.

Liz kept gasping tiny gasps, jumped now and then. Her breathing quickened. Sally wondered if she was actually going to come, backwards like this. The thought excited her so much she lost her rhythm. Liz laughed, patient. Sally tried to catch the rhythm while Liz pressed down on her finger even harder, then seemed to clasp it with herself, let go, clasp again. Sally held her breath for fear of repeating the break in rhythm. She realized that the baby had stopped crying, that Liz's breathing was uneven, that there was absolutely no friction inside Liz now, just a pool her finger swam in, around and around and around and around.

"Hhhhhhhh," breathed Liz in a quiet exhalation. Her tent yawned hugely, then folded down tight. "Sal. Oh God, Sal. Oh."

She held Liz to her, felt their two hearts thump, kissed the side of her forehead. "I love you."

There was silence for a few moments. Sally wondered what her other lovers were doing and smiled into the dark. Had that cab driver quit for the night? Did the prim woman have her orgasm yet? The street musician had taken her sons to a coffeehouse where they were jamming still. The theater-goer — had she put her sturdy heels outside her door for polishing? She felt a pang when she thought of the punk baby-dyke. She hoped the kid had a girlfriend who was sleeping over that very night. Stealthily they were exploring each other's bodies, making sensations of which they'd never dreamed. She began to stroke Liz again.

"That was very nice, Sal."

"Was it, babe?"

"I'd try it on you, but you're too long."

"Maybe you can come up with something else."

"Think so?" asked Liz, leaning over Sally, grinning eyes and teeth faintly visible in the dark.

"You always have before." But Sally was sleepy now, didn't know if she had the steam it would take. She told this to Liz and let her eyes close, snuggled in, content with intimacy.

She wasn't sure, a moment later, if she'd dropped off, and woken again, or if she was dreaming. Had Liz put Bob Dylan on the stereo? How could she know about "Mr. Tamborine Man" tonight? Had that really been a fantasy meter in the cab? She never opened her eyes to ask, though, because it felt too good, what Liz — was it Liz? — was doing, with her mouth, down there.

Sally hugged Liz's head with her thighs to tell her she was awake. Liz was blowing on her, with a warm breath that felt like a Sunday breeze. Just holding her open and blowing up, then down, then up again. Sally began to throb, glad it was Liz's full lips so close to her, not Nicole's thin prim mouth, not the finely drawn lips of the out-of-towner.

Then Liz did something she'd never done before. She thrust her tongue inside Sally, suddenly, and as suddenly, replaced it with her fingers.

"Liz," she said from the shock of it.

"What is it, Sal. Again?"

Sally wondered if the baby-dyke had discovered this

trick yet. "Oooph," she breathed as Liz tongued her repeatedly. "That's an amazing feeling."

"Kind of rough on the tongue muscles, though," Liz said with a laugh.

That laugh. Like the first woman, who had probably long since let her creaking bed go silent. She could see the motion of Liz's head in the dark, moving it back and forth to rest her tongue muscles. Sally felt her own wet parts stretch up. Then Liz's head dropped. Obviously, her tongue had recovered. It moved in just the right ways on just the right places and Sally, out of steam or not, could only follow the feel of Liz's tongue and the hot waves of tension that shook her body.

Her breath became as short as Liz's had been. She knew she was flowing like a fountain. Her body felt like — she wanted to say like it had come home, but how could home be this exciting?

Maybe it was the spring, the lilacs, the rain, the neon lights, the women on the street and her long spring ramble, maybe it was all of that she was feeling as Liz — Sally gripping her shoulders for dear life, a long loud cry at last rolling from her — as Liz brought her home.

RIDING LESSON
Fruitstand IV

It's about time you showed up for work, Bookworm. Five minutes? More like fifteen. What happened, didn't this big red sun come downtown to wake you? You grabbed the express by mistake and had to double back from Woodside Avenue? No? Then maybe we'll read about it in the paper, how Bookworm's train sat in the tunnel for half an hour on the one day she was going to get here early to meet Kathy.

Sure she was by, didn't I tell her my new assistant was drooling to meet her? She grabbed her break, the boss hollering and all, and you're not even here. I need you to unload some more of those crates off the truck on the double. That sun's not cooling down any. It looks like July in the city for sure today.

You finished unloading? Talk about slow. If it weren't for my back creaking and groaning inside like the old Third Avenue El, I'd have them all on display by now. Never mind did Kathy help me throw my back out last night. What do you think, we've all got one-track minds like you?

Now what put me in mind of the El like that? I'll bet I haven't thought of it in years. Seems like there was a lot less crime then, though, having some of the cars out in the open like that. Am I right? Why, me and Dagmar — that was it. Dagmar Allen. Kathy waited on her yesterday.

Yeah, yeah, I'll tell you about Dagmar, but I want you on that sprayer pretty constant today, you understand? I'm glad we caught the refrigeration problem in April instead of waiting for the heat. I can't believe Dag and me used to go into the city to get cool. We could have gone to an R.K.O. right in Queens, but was that good enough for us? No, we went to Saturday matinees on Broadway where her dad could get tickets. Lucky for me he was a stagehand or I might never have discovered the shows.

Dag? She was a classmate at the sister school. We were the tallest in our class and always got put at the back of the line together.

Hey! Don't forget, extra mist on the apricots. They wither up faster than a subway rider on July third.

Did I tell you? We're shutting down on the Fourth. Didn't even sell a pint of strawberries for shortcake last year or the year before, and Kathy's restaurant's closing too. We thought we'd take a bus out to the stables, nose around. No, I won't ride with my back like this. Besides, I never thought it was exactly right, people using animals to get around. I mean, who do we think we are? It'd mostly be to see Dag again. Kathy says she hasn't changed a bit.

From what? From that great tall adventurous girl in jeans and a work shirt, the one I used to ride the subways with. From the tomboy kid who couldn't sit still in school and taught me to ride horses. From the long-legged girl in a plaid skirt, knee socks and white blouse with a Peter Pan collar who used to shoot hoops with me and one of the nuns.

What did I know from queer at that age, Bookworm. No, we never did anything together except play like two wild things unleashed from the classrooms. After school Dag would tear off her skirt first chance she got. "I feel like a sissy in it," she always said. We saw *Teahouse of the August Moon* on Broadway that year after passing Dag off as a guy to get her in. Women in pants weren't allowed.

What are you trying to do, kiddo, drown the poor nectarines? Pay attention to what you're doing. Here, dry them off with this. Then go on up to the Korean market and get me some prices. Let's make sure they don't undersell us today. It's easier to keep the customers than to win them back. Am I right? And don't stop at that bookshop to buy a paperback. You want a story, I'll tell you more about Dag.

That was quick. I should've figured — you want more story. Let me see that list. Bananas. Go mark down the bananas. And let's do a special on the cherries. I got a good price, but the way you're misting, they'll rot with the nectarines. Yeah, yeah, we'll get back to Dagmar. Are you playing anthropology student again? And who said you could stop for batteries on fruitstand time? You know I hate that darned tape recorder.

Dag Allen was pretty wild for a girl in the fifties. We were all supposed to grow up to look like poor Mamie Eisenhower. Have you seen pictures? Permed hair puffed out around our ears, skirts to our calves, clunky black shoes and girdles to keep us in one place. Dag was wonderful, a rebel like James Dean. No other girl got away with wearing jeans. I tried to persuade my mother, but you'd think I'd declared World War III, which we were waiting for, by the way. We had air raid drills all the time at school. The horrible clanging bell would go off and the sisters would herd us into the hallways where we sat on the floor, heads down, hands across the back of our necks, like prisoners.

I suppose you're right, we were prisoners of the cold war, Bookworm, but Dag and me, at the end of the line, poked and giggled together. We were just little tomboys even at sixteen. The ugly things in life weren't real to us. Yet.

About once a month I'd go home with her. She lived half a block from a pint-sized stable. Dag was head over heels with those horses. She'd hung around since grade school, helping Jack, the owner, clean out stalls, learning everything she could. When she got tall enough Jack hired her to give the little kids pony rides at the park. In exchange, she got to ride whenever she wanted. She took to horse life like berries to the sun. Instead of this big gawky girl with an oldfashioned braid, Dag was like a real cowgirl, pitching hay or riding across North Hempstead Turnpike into the park, braid tucked under a straw cowboy hat.

I felt like her greenhorn sidekick, bouncing up and down on my saddle. Fruit I knew, but only rich people rode horses in the city. I even got to wear my first pair of jeans with her. It was worth it, just for that.

Even after the summer when she changed like a caterpillar to a butterfly — in reverse as far as I was concerned — she had a style no one could copy. Even when she joined the hoody seniors and wore makeup and short skirts she walked like an actor in drag through a crowd of extras. What she did, she switched best friends to be with this jazzy gal Charlotte Hogan, the leader of the girl hoods.

Charlotte Hogan was interested in boys, boys, boys. She'd lipstick hearts and initials inside the bathroom stalls. The C.H. always stayed the same, but the other initials changed faster than you can sell cranberries in November. I started seeing Dag's name up there too. The initials inside her heart were always Charlotte's hand-me-downs.

Now, I knew how Dag felt about guys. They weren't very smart. They were too big. They smelled bad. They called her horseface, then tried to cage rides from her. I tried to tell her they weren't all bad, but nothing doing. How could she stoop to dressing up for them? Going out with them? She couldn't have liked it — because am I right — Bookworm, deep down inside you know when a woman's one of your own. Even in ribbons and lace — you still know. There was only one explanation about Dag. She did it to get close to Charlotte.

Speaking of ribbons, we have a couple of gift baskets to make up. One for a customer, but I want you to do one for Fred, he can't come by these days. HIV. Yeah, I miss his dumb jokes. I'll take it by on my way home, catch him up on the neighborhood dish.

I really missed Dag. She didn't shoot hoops anymore, she skipped school half the time, she didn't even go by the stables. I know because I went over there and talked to Jack. "Just like that!" he says, snapping his fingers. "She's here one day and gone the next. If you ask me, she's in love."

In 1954 I'd never heard the word gay. All I knew was to laugh at people like Fred, with their antiques and poodles, and to laugh at women truck drivers. But now my Dag had a crush the size of a watermelon on Charlotte. I could see it in her eyes, in the way she'd bend to talk to the girl, like a guy would his date. It got my wheels turning, am I right? Dag went on dates to get close to Charlotte, maybe they doubled. Maybe she liked making out with boys who'd touched Charlotte. Maybe her and Charlotte compared notes and things got steamy between them. Maybe they practiced. Maybe I wished I could get steamy with Dag.

You know how it is, having those queer shadows in your head, knowing this stuff and running as far as you can from it? Hey, nice basket, Bookworm. Add some cherries to Fred's, will you? We used to see who could spit the pits farthest. I'll bet I could win these days. I hate it, though. Sometimes I hate what life brings to us, take it or leave it, no moneyback guarantees.

One day in June I go into home-room a little late — Dag and Charlotte and me were all in Sister Adelaide's room — and there's this whispering, giggling and staring going on. I'm surprised to see Dag and Charlotte aren't in the middle of the ruckus. Charlotte's looking at her nails, the floor, out the window, lips thin and tight as a customer who just found a worm in her apple. Dag's bright pink in the face, scribbling in a notebook, looking more than ever like she's in costume for a stage part that's going to end. Charlotte's not talking to Dag. These two are like Siamese strawberries since September, am I right? Sister Adelaide comes in just then and slaps her ruler against the desk twice to quiet the class, but you can feel the excitement like slow boiling water in a canning pot.

Later, in gym, I crowd into the bathroom with all the other curious girls. Somebody'd wiped out the boy's initials in Charlotte's heart and wrote "C.H. loves D.A."

Maybe we were innocent parochial school girls, but somebody drew another heart next to the first one and wrote "C.H. *Licks* D.A." That was the only sex ed lesson I ever had in sister school. I can still hear the squeals as one girl explained it to the next.

"Down there, it means," says my tutor, embarrassed, fluttering. *"Ugh!"* she adds to cover her excitement.

Was it true, what they were saying? Or was it just that pack instinct, turning on the one they sensed was different? I didn't see Charlotte talk to Dag the rest of that week. If she loved Dag, she wasn't abdicating her throne for her. By Friday, Charlotte, in her tight plaid skirt and little girl's blouse over her pointy bra, had won back her place as the queen of the hoods. Dag didn't make it to that last week of school.

I craned my neck watching for Dag at graduation, feeling my tassel bob around like her braid. At practice she'd been assigned the seat next to mine. Finally, just as the school orchestra finishes tuning, she marches in the door. Sister Adelaide tries to stop her, but Dag brushes her off and climbs over me to sit. Sister Adelaide reaches across me to tug on her arm. I thought it was because Dag had missed the last week's classes.

Dag wouldn't budge. The principal started her speech in a little voice. The sister gave up. Dag passed me a note. *I'm sorry, Henny,* I read. *I must have lost my mind all year. I guess I didn't want to be me for a while there, but I learned my lesson.* Then she opened her robe and I saw why Sister Adelaide was so red-faced furious. Dag was wearing her horse clothes to graduation, the jeans and the plaid shirt and boots. She smelled of stable. Delicious.

You're cheering already? Wait till I tell you this. Because of being tallest, Dag's the last girl to go up. I've got my diploma and I'm leaving the stage. I hear a gasp and I look back to watch Dag accept her diploma in drag. You understand, I didn't see it like that then. I stop on the stairs when I see she's tossed her mortarboard and is pulling her cowboy hat out from under her wide-open robe.

Can you believe it? In 1954! She was telling those

girls they were right! She was what she was and proud!

Well, I'm stock still as she comes down the stairs, staring, ready to protect my head when the bomb falls. She grabs my arm and lets out a whoop, dragging me up the aisle with her. She doesn't turn into our row of seats though. She goes on to the door, stops, turns around, says, "I have to get back to work at the stable. Jack hired me full time! Come by and see me!" And she was gone.

I wanted with all my heart to fly out that door after her, but my family's in the audience and we have to make a living in the neighborhood. I decided it could wait a day.

It waited a couple of weeks, to tell you the truth. See, I wasn't ready to come out. That would take a few more years. Sure, we went riding a few times. When she brought a girlfriend around to the shop I was confused. As much as I admired Dag, I was scared to be seen with a woman who always wore jeans and had a girl on her arm.

But, like I say, after all these years Kathy ran into her the other day. Kathy used to be one of those girls on Dag's arm. So things have come full swing. Dag bought the stable from Jack. I think it's time to go on out there with a major fruit basket and tell Dag the end of my story. With Kathy on my arm.

HANUKKAH AT A BAR
At A Bar XII

Great patches of clouds like assemblies of white smoke puffs filled the sky. The street was silent, as if cold muffled Soho. Sally the bartender, tall and blonde, stood outside Cafe Femmes, just beyond the lavender awning, her breath turning to steam. Head back, she watched the clouds drift by, sniffed the frozen, sooty air. Were they snow clouds, or did they just look like soft heaps of the stuff poised, waiting like the whole city for Christmas?

No, thought Sally, as she returned to the warm bar, not the whole city. Not Liz, her lover and partner at Cafe Femmes. Liz and the other Jews of the city weren't waiting for Christmas, but quietly readying for Hanukkah, which would start Sunday, two days away. She picked up the bar rag she'd left on a table and moved around the smoky-smelling room, wiping down every surface. The lunch crowd was neater than the night crowd, but there were pizza stains, dried beer foam, sticky Coke spills. Gabby, who normally took care of the restaurant business, had left early for a doctor appointment and wouldn't be back till the dinner hour.

Hanukkah. It had never been a big deal before. She scrubbed finger smudges off the plastic window of the electronic game. Liz always said she was proud to be a Jew. In their first years together Sally had never failed to give her a present at least on the first of the eight-day celebration. But Hanukkah reminded Liz of her family and she hadn't encouraged Sally. She'd cried enough, Liz had said, over her stubborn, nearly Orthodox father's edict that she never set foot in his home again. Over what she'd lost by being gay. Eventually they'd marked the holiday only by placing a menorah on the bar.

But last spring, for the first time in the fifteen years since Liz had come out to her parents, Mrs. Marks had called to invite Liz to join them for Passover. Liz. Not Liz and Sally. Liz had refused. Now her mother had tried again, wanting her for Hanukkah. And Liz had been overwrought, sleepless, ever since, poised like the snow clouds, wanting to fall back into her family's arms, but wanting also to be her whole self. She was Sally's lover, she said, not just her father's daughter.

A voice called, "Guess I'll have to help myself."

Sally jumped, knocked out of her worried trance. LilyAnn Lee was so tall she was making a habit of silencing the cowbells with her hand before the door hit them.

"You trying to give me heart failure?" asked Sally, rounding the bar, trailing her fingers on its polished wood.

LilyAnn Lee reached across the bar, set the seltzer hose back and lowered herself to her stool. She was six feet tall, solid-looking, her skin an even, glowing dark brown. She crossed her legs, set her elbows on the bar and leaned seductively toward Sally. Her fingernail polish was a shocking metallic magenta, her dangling earrings flashed in the light. A heady perfume filled Sally's nostrils. She shook her head. It had always amazed her how utterly feminine this big woman could make herself. She remembered being struck by that even the first time she'd seen LilyAnn Lee, a freshman entering during Sally's senior year. She'd been sure LilyAnn was gay until she'd next seen her — on the arm of a male athlete.

"You *know* I don't care for those cowbells ringing so close to my sensitive ear," said LilyAnn Lee.

Sally grinned and suggested, "Stoop."

"*I* do not stoop for any white girl's cowbells. Not LilyAnn Lee, M.B.A." She grinned too. "How's my old pal Sal?"

"You mean besides the heart attack?"

"Come to think of it, you *are* kind of pale."

"I *am*?" Sally asked, turning to look in the mirror.

"Compared to *what* is the question."

Sally turned back. "Very funny."

"What do you have in the nonalcoholic line?" asked LilyAnn.

"A Lavender Julie?"

"That sticky-sweet grape thing Gabby thrives on? Not for me."

"The Jefferson Lime *Squeeze*?"

"Say *what*?"

She wiped the bar top between them, grinning again. This would make up for the paleface routine. "You heard me."

"Don't tell me Jefferson is back in town. And not drinking? Well, my, my, will wonders never cease."

Sally filled her in on their old schoolmate, the woman athlete who'd finally brought LilyAnn Lee out.

"What do you call it? A Jefferson Lime *Squeeze*? I'll bet she likes that name. Let me try one — it must be good if it's keeping Jefferson herself off the sauce." Sally poured lime and white grape juices over crushed ice. "You tell her I'm putting fires out now, not starting them in the girls' dorm?" LilyAnn asked.

She nodded. "And that you finished graduate school before you joined the Fire Department." Despite her sardonic expression, she could tell LilyAnn still cared what Jefferson thought. Kindly, she conceded, "She was impressed."

"Mmm-uh!" said LilyAnn, sucking in her cheeks as she tasted the tart drink. She didn't have to work again until Monday night, she told Sally, and settled in at the bar for the afternoon. Customers came and went as they talked about their old school days. A

138

little later Julie, who managed a florist shop uptown, made her weekly stop with flowers. Sally and LilyAnn worked together, arranging them in little vases on the tables, indulging in their spring-like scents.

"I'm back!" Gabby announced unnecessarily as she slammed the door against the cowbells. Short, stocky, with graying hair brushed back from her forehead, she rushed to the counter and grabbed an apron. "Hey, Big Lil," she said as she began her preparations.

"That was a long doctor appointment," Sally commented with concern. Gabby was never late.

"I — ah — had to make a stop."

"Did she say you're okay?" They all went to Dr. Sterne, who frequented an uptown bar, but promised she'd visit Cafe Femmes sometime.

"Yeah," said Gabby brusquely, as if completely, uncharacteristically absorbed in her work.

Her silence worried Sally. She lay down the wet bar rag and crossed to stand next to Gabby, watching as she deftly cut salad vegetables, sharp wooden knife in her square fingers. Her eyes looked red, but then she'd just finished a neat stack of fragrant onions. Gabby was only forty. It couldn't be anything that serious, could it?

"Shit!" Gabby said.

Sally saw the blood spurt to the surface of Gabby's thumb, saw her drop the knife, the endive. Then, holding a towel against her cut, Gabby began to cry. Sally put an arm around her shoulder and patted it awkwardly. Gabby cried on, quietly, lifting the bloody towel two-handed to her face to wipe the tears.

"What's going on here?" LilyAnn asked. Sally shrugged, but LilyAnn seemed to take it all in at once and in a moment had a strip of clean cloth around Gabby's thumb. She held Gabby tight against her breasts. "You're going to have to tell somebody, Little Gab," she said with a soothing tone Sally imagined her using on survivors of fires. "Do you have to be hospitalized?"

Gabby shook her head against LilyAnn's breasts and managed to say, "I don't know. But I hate it, I hate it. Why do bodies have to wear out?" Then she sobbed more.

"What *is* it, Gab?" Sally urged. "You know we're family. Have you told Amaretto?"

Gabby nodded. "I stopped there after the tests."

"Tests?" asked Sally and LilyAnn simultaneously.

"It's arrhythmia. It means irregular heartbeat. It could be nothing. But I could die!"

"Oh-ho," Sally joked. "The junk food years are over."

But she felt a coldness around her own heart. Not Gabby. She was finally very, very sober, had a job that suited her, and was with a fine lover.

"Doc Sterne sent me down for more tests today. I see her Monday for the results."

Sally left LilyAnn to minister to Gabby and served a customer at the bar.

She could see through the plate glass window, beyond the backwards words, "CAFE FEMMES," that dusk had come.

She moved to the door and stepped outside.

There was an icy chill to the air that made her flesh feel raw. A lone truck was unloading at the warehouse across the street, its exhaust inescapable. She coughed. With a clang, someone rolled shut the metal door on a loading dock. The city had a feeling of impermanence to it. Cities, bodies, did wear out. Even the little tree newly planted in front of Cafe Femmes struggled to live. She looked up and saw those smoke-puff clouds still hanging, still full, waiting and waiting — for what?

She sighed, tired, and went back in. She'd lost sleep too, with Liz not sleeping. Should she tell Liz about Gabby, or did she have enough on her mind?

But just then Liz arrived, cheeks red from the cold, a soft, pale green scarf wrapped around her neck. She moved as quickly as ever, a woman who meant business, but Sally could see the tension in her limbs, the tautness of her facial muscles, the darkness under her eyes. They entered the bar together. She unwound the scarf from Liz's neck with great tenderness. Liz brought the smell of home with her.

"How's it going?" she asked.

"My mother called again." Liz's voice was hoarse. She must have been crying too. Sometimes, Sally thought as she drew a pitcher of cold beer and smiled automatically at the woman who'd ordered, sometimes it seemed as if the whole world was a cloud, filled with moisture, and everyone must take a turn in overflowing. She returned to Liz's side. "I asked her if I could bring you. My mate. My companion. My chosen family."

Sally could tell. "She said no."

"She said my father had come a long way. That I should compromise too. That I was wrong to want the whole schmear at once."

"And you said —"

Liz became agitated. She was polishing her glasses ferociously. " 'All at once?' I said to her. 'You're not

141

going to be around forever, Ma. I want my family all at once, yes, and now. All at once,' " she repeated with sarcasm. "After fifteen years of not seeing the inside of my family home." The Marks family owned a brownstone in Brooklyn and Liz sometimes remembered it aloud, room by room, when she came home in the early morning and climbed in beside the already sleeping Sally, who'd wrap her long legs around Liz and hold her, breathing that home scent, half-dreaming, half-listening, until Liz's brownstone became part of her own dreams, as if she'd grown up there too.

"You're not going."

"I asked for another day to talk to you about it."

"Right down to the wire."

"I need to know how *you* feel, Sal. What it would mean to you not to be there."

"Hey, I've lived without Hanukkah for forty-one years now."

"Not good enough, babe. I don't want one of your unfeeling WASP answers."

Sally shrugged, and went to serve a group of office workers on their way home from work. What could she do? She'd been brought up to think of emotions as the equivalent of something you did in the bathroom. Sure she had them, but to lay them down on the bar, or even think about them much, wasn't something she was good at. Sometimes, to tell the truth, Liz carried on a little too much. There she was now, hugging Gabby to death, holding her hand, making much of what might be nothing. She'd have Gabby crying into her endives and sunchokes all night.

142

She started to leave as soon as Liz was ready to begin her shift. Didn't even kiss her good-bye.

"Are you mad?" Liz asked, catching up with her at the door.

"Mad?" asked Sally, surprised. Now Liz was making another crisis. The office workers were singing "Happy Birthday" noisily and she had to talk over them. "Why should I be mad?"

"Don't shout at me!" Liz said, turning away with tears in her eyes.

Sally stood tall, unbending, and plunged into the chilled air. A web of emotions covered Cafe Femmes tonight — fear and conflict, longing and self-pity extending into every corner. She was glad to leave it behind. And sorry. She decided to stay in the dark, hushed neighborhood.

"Wait up, girl!" she heard behind her.

It was LilyAnn Lee loping toward her.

"Which way you heading?"

Sally shrugged again. "Just away."

"Walk with me to the firehouse. I have to pick up my laundry."

LilyAnn had discovered Cafe Femmes when she was assigned to the local station. They walked there in silence now, bundled into themselves against the cold, the six-foot black woman, her Afro trimmed down for safety at work, and the tall blonde who could tell her ears were reddening in the stinging wind.

The rest of the company was out on a fire. Sally looked around the drab firehouse and wondered what LilyAnn's life could be like, among all these men.

"Pretty lonely," LilyAnn said later, over a red

sauce smelling powerfully of oregano at Sally's favorite candle lit restaurant in Little Italy. They'd stopped at the service laundry around the corner first. "Some of them hate me. Some of them want to get in my pants. In between are one or two who respect me for what I am, who've watched me work and know I'm there for them on a fire, because that's my job, keeping lives going the best way I can."

"My job is cushy compared to that."

"You shitting me? Remember, I worked out there in that business world before I got this job. It's as dangerous as fire-fighting. You just get burnt in different ways. *I* wouldn't want to work six days a week, every week of the year, put up with organized crime threats and every other racket there is. Look at the risks you take with your money, your security, sitting ducks for queer-bashers. I wouldn't want to listen to the gay kids' problems. Watch the love and the loss, the happiness that's here one day, gone the next. The waste. So many of those kids don't know how lucky they are to have life. They're drinking, drugging it away, like it's some miserable sentence they have to get through. No, I'd rather go out on a fire where I know what to expect, what to do when I get there, watch people appreciate life."

"Is that why you went with the Fire Department? To save lives?"

LilyAnn's eyes sparked like Liz's did when she talked about the old brownstone. "You know, growing up in my part of the city was never dull. Even the bad things brought an excitement that livened up the day-to-day drudgery of my mother making ends meet, of me fighting my way through that hard, ugly

144

school, because she told me it was my ticket to living better. So when we had a fire, even though it scared me to death, I'd be running out there with everyone else to watch the red engines, the men in black, all the commotion. The howling sirens, that burning smoky smell wasn't all bad, for me. And those men in black, they were heroes. Time after time they'd save a neighbor, a schoolmate, someone's family or dog. It made me live my little life on a higher plane for a few hours, thinking how those people had gotten a second chance, dreaming how I'd live my second chance now, this day here." LilyAnn, dark eyes full of light, joked as if to cover up her high ideals. "How if I could save lives like that people might even be glad, for once, I'd been born so tall. I *knew* there had to be a reason I stuck out like the Chrysler building in a bunch of tenements."

They'd drunk a half bottle of wine with dinner, and Sally found herself loving LilyAnn Lee, feeling close and trusting. She lay her hand on LilyAnn's firm arm and told her about Liz's brownstone, and Hanukkah. "It's okay with me if she goes," Sally concluded. "I *expect* to be left out. I'm not real family, I'm not the right religion, and it's one of those things you swallow when you're queer."

"Swallow? If you're swallowing it so easily, why are you crying?"

"Because of Liz. She's always making me have emotions." She dried her eyes with the paper napkin. It hadn't really been a cry, just a few wine-induced tears.

"*Making* you have emotions?"

She nodded. "I'm fine on my own. But she's always asking what I feel."

145

LilyAnn was looking strangely at her. "You know you're talking shit, don't you, girl? You sound like Jefferson," she said, "back when she thought she was a mental Hercules. Nothing reached her. Not cheating on her girl to get me, not bringing me out and then dumping me when she was done, not smashing herself in that car accident. Took me a long time to see her trick. She drowned it all in the juice. What do you do with your feelings, Sal?"

"You mean you think Liz is right? I do feel more than I know I do?"

The waitress brought them each a tortoni, but food no longer appealed to Sally. "Inside," she said, after a silence, "I guess I agree with Liz's dad. It's his home. He doesn't want an outsider there, sharing in an intimate family ritual. Even if I were a man, I'd still be as outsider as you can get."

"Now," LilyAnn said between bites, "thanks to you I know how *he* feels, but I still don't know what you're feeling."

"But I don't *care*." She passed her dessert across the table.

LilyAnn took a break between portions. She stretched her legs into the aisle of the emptying restaurant and locked her hands behind her head. "I am remembering," LilyAnn began in a trance-like voice, "remembering what it felt like when I thought I was an outsider."

"You don't feel like an outsider anymore?"

"A miracle, isn't it? In this long black body of mine. In this queerness that I love. No, I don't feel sad any more, almost ever. I don't feel at the mercy of anyone else's emotions — my mother muttering into her glass how hard life is, my teachers'

146

frustration with how we ghet-to kids didn't learn the way we s'posed to, my friends' rage at not being able to have what they wanted in this white world. I stayed an outsider as long as they counted more than I did. When I learned, right after Jefferson left me, to be my own friend, to reach inside me, I became an insider. Life opened up. It's a big thing, life. And I want to stuff as much into it, or as much of me into it, as I can. If somebody doesn't want me around, that's his problem, he's the outsider."

They paid the check and went into the night. "I don't want to go back yet," Sally said. So they walked up to Greenwich Village, past the brightly lit shops, the music spilling from dark clubs, through the noise of panhandlers, drug dealers, tourists and oblivious natives. It felt warmer in the heat of the Village, in the midst of so many smells — expresso, pizza, marijuana, sandlewood incense. "So *that's* how I feel, like an outsider," Sally said.

"I'd stare at those big red trucks," LilyAnn responded, "and the men with their equipment, their know-how, their *guts* and belief in life, everyone's life, and I'd think, back when I was an outsider, I'll *never* be able to do that."

"I know that feeling. You don't count. If the Chief of the Fire Department doesn't think you belong —"

"If Liz's father doesn't think you belong —"

Sally stopped at an alleyway. "But I *don't* want to go to the brownstone for Hanukkah. I *don't* want to feel like a sore thumb, an intruder, an unbeliever."

"So don't."

"Oh," said Sally, looking into LilyAnn's eyes, and then up the alleyway as if she'd just found the path she'd been looking for. "Oh," she said again. "So *that's* what I really want — not to go. But I do want to share the holy days with Liz. They're part of her, part of us. Even her parents, we need to share them too."

They began walking back, south.

LilyAnn remained silent.

"I *want* to be included in her celebration. That's why I always give her presents. If only there were a way to equalize her parents and me. So it's not all in their ballpark. So I belong too. I want to be able to enjoy what we do share, not feel awful about it."

LilyAnn lay an arm across her shoulders and gave her a sideways hug as they walked. *"That's* a Jefferson Squeeze, hold the lime," LilyAnn said, laughing.

Sunday, as part of the compromise she worked out with her family, Liz went to celebrate the first night of Hanukkah at her parents' brownstone — without Sally.

But the second night, Monday, when the bar was closed, her family kept its part of the bargain and visited Cafe Femmes to light two of the candles in Liz and Sally's menorah. Liz had invited Gabby, who darted in after her doctor's visit, and LilyAnn Lee, on her way to work, in uniform.

"What, the Fire Department?" asked Mr. Marks. "I *knew* it must be against some code to light Hanukkah candles in a bar." He was white-haired, with Liz's dark eyes, but his thick still-black eyebrows made him fierce-looking.

"Just don't let me hear the word *shiksa* out of his mouth," Liz had muttered to Sally. She'd come back to work from Brooklyn on Sunday, relieved it was over, that first meeting with her father, full of hope and anger all at the same time. Tonight she wore the long velveteen skirt she saved for weddings and funerals. Sally wore a pantsuit from her days in an office and could hardly breathe. Gabby had chosen her best black overalls and a bright pink shirt.

At last Sally was hearing the fabled interchanges in person.

"*You* gave her a goy name — Elizabeth," accused Mr. Marks in an undertone.

"Quiet, Abe. *You* wanted her to fit in the modern world," Mrs. Marks whispered loudly.

"Not *this* modern."

Liz had made coffee for the baked goods her mother brought. Its smell, as well as the parents, transformed the bar into something close in intent to what Liz had always said she wanted it to be, but at the same time not as close because of the nervous energy gathered in the air. As they assembled to light the candles there was a knock at the door.

"Closed!" shouted Mr. Marks, obviously on edge.

Liz winced.

"It's probably Amaretto," Gabby said, bustling to the door to let her in.

"What happened?" Amaretto cried, gathering Gabby into her arms. Amaretto's grandmother, Nanny, who spent a great deal of time with the couple, had come in behind her granddaughter. "What did Dr. Sterne have to say?" Amaretto demanded.

Sally felt herself shrink. The last thing they needed in front of Liz's parents was this display of lesbian affection.

Gabby looked toward Liz as if to apologize.

"Gabby had heart tests, Ma, Dad," Liz explained. "She came here straight from the doctor's."

"So why didn't she say right away?" Mrs. Marks asked. "We're some kind of monsters?"

Gabby hung her head. Pretty Amaretto, in her thrift store fake fur, kept an arm around her lover's shoulder. "I don't think —" Gabby said.

"Tell!" bellowed Mr. Marks. He lowered his voice. "I have a little heart problem myself."

"I'm okay. I have 'premature systoles'," Gabby said with labored pronunciation. "That's extra heartbeats." Amaretto grabbed her in a hug again.

"That's exactly what I have," said Mr. Marks. "Not to worry," he said reassuringly, "so long as you take care of yourself and keep healthy. Don't drink," he warned, naming preventive measures on his fingers. "Exercise, don't smoke, and," he poked the last finger toward her stomach, "maybe lose a little weight?"

Gabby laughed. "That's the cheapest second opinion I could have gotten!"

They shook hands. Gabby introduced him to Amaretto and Nanny. Sally looked at Liz, then at LilyAnn Lee in amazement as Gabby and Mr. Marks talked on about their symptoms. Amaretto was still holding Gabby's hand. They'd only been lovers since October and were obviously crazy about each other. Was that why Mrs. Marks went to stand by her husband, and took his hand too? Soon Nanny engaged her in conversation. Mr. Marks glanced down as he talked, looking at his fingers interlaced with his wife's. Then over to Gabby and Amaretto's hands. Then to Nanny, beaming and nodding, apparently completely comfortable. He scratched his chin.

"Okay, okay," said Liz, before her father had a

chance to decide he didn't want to be a part of it all. "Did you two come to light the candles or to hang out in our bar all night?"

Everyone laughed.

Liz handed a box of matches to her father.

"Wait!" cried Gabby. She skipped over to the jukebox and fussed with it briefly. In a moment the room filled with the sounds of "Sunrise, Sunset" from *Fiddler On the Roof.*

"Oy," said Liz.

"Tacky, little Gab," said LilyAnn. "Very tacky."

"Huh?"

LilyAnn folded her arms. "Would you come to my family celebration and play *Porgy and Bess*?"

"It's okay, it's okay," said Mr. Marks. "Let her celebrate her good health any way she wants. Maybe Mrs. Marks will teach you the hora. Good exercise."

Gabby's face was red, but she said, "I want to feel the spirit. This isn't a funeral, it's a holiday! What's a holiday without music? After this scare, I want *everything* to count for me."

Laughing with the rest, Mr. Marks turned to the candles. "This is not the real thing," he began. "It's a little bit ecumenical. So you can understand." The others ranged around the bar. "At Hanukkah the Jews celebrate their freedom to worship. No, we celebrate freedom of religion. For everyone." He gestured toward them all.

Sally's hand stole to Liz's. They were here, all of them, because Sally had decided, and said, it was what she wanted. Liz had thought Hanukkah at the bar was a fantastic idea. And now it felt so good.

She needed to touch Liz's soft hand and feel close. She reminded herself there was nothing wrong with showing what she felt.

Mr. Marks went on. "As we light each candle, we symbolize the growth of faith. Always, my wife and I, we have prayed to be reunited with our child, Elizabeth. Life is too short, like Gabby said, to lose anything we have." He reached out his hand to his daughter and she moved toward him, still holding Sally's hand, pulling her along. Sally balked. Liz tugged. Mr. Marks' hand wavered, began to drop, but after Liz's mother jerked obviously at his coat, he steadied the hand, pulled Liz, and Sally, to himself. "Always, my God humbles me, teaches me through His will," Mr. Marks said, head bowed.

Then he looked up at Liz, and for the first time, at Sally. She imagined this time she really did look pale, like Friday when LilyAnn teased her. But LilyAnn wouldn't say a thing, she knew, because she had seen the tears rolling down those broad brown cheeks. It made her want to cry too. She swallowed hard.

"Once more then," said Mr. Marks, "as at the first Hanukkah, we celebrate a miracle of faith." He turned, said some words in Hebrew and lit the two candles.

"Tomorrow," he said then, turning back to Liz and Sally, "will you both," and his voice sounded choked here, as if the word *both* came hard, very hard, "will you both come for the lighting, to Brooklyn?"

"If we can cover the bar," Sally answered, stopping herself from obsequiously thanking him for his acceptance. She wanted an out should she choose to use it.

After coffee and pastries, her parents hugged Liz and shook hands all around. Outside, Liz walked them to their car. Sally stood just beyond Cafe Femmes' awning, looking up. The temperature had risen and the puffy snow clouds were gone for now. The sky would weep another day.

She stubbornly kept her eyes skyward as LilyAnn joined her. It wouldn't do to look down and let all those tears fall out of her eyes. But then LilyAnn Lee put an arm around her shoulder and squeezed her tight. Sally, feeling like a cloud whose time has come, looked wetly down.

INEZ

When Inez walked down from the hills through town at night, it was as if the streets rumbled under her feet. Big-boned, hefty and solid, she felt wholly alive, hardy and powerful. If she could hold a tune she'd bellow out a song with all twenty-eight years of life in her.

The fog had been thin in the hills, but close to the river it filled the streets. There were no lamp posts in this part of town, just the occasional warehouse floodlight at a side door. She rumbled on, sucking the damp night air into her lungs as if it nourished her.

When she opened the door of the bar the blast of heat and music were almost enough to knock her backwards onto the street. The bouncer, a man even taller than she was, irritably motioned for her to pull the door shut. She exhaled all that night air, all that confidence, and dug in her pocket for the $2.00 cover. He wrapped her money around a roll of bills. Saturday night at the River's Edge Tavern they packed them in.

Inez looked for a seat. There was one table empty, jutting onto the dance floor. She took it and, feeling more and more like a swollen sore thumb, sat for twenty-five minutes before the waitress brought her a Coke. That was a relief, to have something to do with her hands and with her eyes. She didn't smoke and she was embarrassed to stare at the dancers, or at the sitters who were staring at the dancers and at one another.

Once inside the Edge, every week, she wanted nothing more than to get out, to be back on the streets, filling up to her full size, yet invisible in the night. She'd tried leaving and then returning, but the bouncer charged her every time. She didn't have money to waste — she was an assistant cook at the mental hospital. Whenever a cook quit she thought she'd get the promotion, but they always hired a man over her.

She watched the bubbles in her soda. She sipped. The crowd played the Chiffons, the Chantels, the Capris, and some of the mushy hits she loved. When "Moon River" came on she longed to dance in some woman's arms, but when "Lollipops and Roses" played, she wanted to cry.

It was this big body of hers that was the problem. She'd always liked her strong arms and legs. The shadow of a mustache that had been getting more obvious since her late teens ran in her family. She was just short of six feet and her mom and dad bragged of her strength and robustness. But who'd bring the likes of her lollipops and roses?

She peeked at the dancers. Now that one gave her the shivers. They called her Kookie after the TV character because she was always combing her hair, just like him. She drifted into a daydream: Kookie asks her to dance to "Moon River." Kookie suddenly grows almost a foot as she leads the way to the floor. Inez lays her cheek on Kookie's shoulder. "You're so easy to lead," Kookie tells her after hours of dancing. Outside, Kookie opens the door to her midnight-blue Mercury Monterey and carefully closes Inez in. Like magic, they're in Kookie's wide soft bed and Inez is being undressed. She lies back, an adored, trusting kitten, while Kookie caresses her everywhere.

"Hey," Kookie shouted at her over the din of the bar. "We're going to do a stroll line here. You want to move this table back?"

"Okey-doke," Inez said, lifting the table with its heavy metal stand and moving it one-handed.

"She's strong," said Kookie's girl.

"She's a moose," said Kookie, a little too loud.

Inez scuttled behind her table, trying to hide the red of her face. *I've got to get out of here,* she thought, but felt too conspicuous to leave. If she did, where else could she hope to meet a woman to love?

"You should've punched her out," said a small voice from the table beside her.

She whipped around and glared toward the voice.

"Sorry," said the woman. "Don't look at *me* that way. I didn't call you any names."

Inez lowered her eyes. "Sorry," she said too, her throat clogged with tears.

"I mean it. Why don't you go put her lights out?"

"Yeah," said a stunningly handsome gay man beside the woman. "I'd do it for you, but I might ruin my nylon."

She looked down at his crossed legs and saw that under his khakis he really was in stockings. He twisted his calf to show her the black seam.

She grinned despite herself. "I wish I could wear those," she said, hearing how incongruous such a desire sounded in her bass voice.

"Do it, sweetie. It's a gas."

"They'd look goofy on me," she told him. The spunky woman was stripping the label from her beer bottle, frowning. She was pretty, Inez thought, with tiny bones and baby-fine hair almost to her shoulders, dimples and delicate features.

The stroll line was long, each couple self-consciously taking its moment in the spotlight. Some giggled, some were intensely cool. Kookie combed her hair all the way down the line. Her girl, in tight black skirt and spit curls, rolled her eyes at her antics.

"How come you two aren't dancing?" she asked the pretty woman and the handsome man, just to make conversation. The woman's scowl came up like a cop's nightstick in a raid and she used her head to gesture behind the boy. Inez winced when she saw that he was sitting in a wheelchair. The table hid its arms. "Sorry," she said. "I'm so used to them at work I never even noticed. Did you have polio or what?"

He picked up his left pant leg and showed her the brace. "That's why I dress the other one up. Cinderella and her ugly stepsister. My name's Walter. This is Cherensky. She hates her first name."

"Don't you dare," warned Cherensky in her little girl voice.

"*I* think it's you, Daisy. I don't know why you hate it."

The stroll ended and a fast song came on. "I won't mind if you two dance," Walter said.

Cherensky used her severely clipped fingernails to scrape the bottle bare. Inez sighed. Another matchmaker, pairing her with a woman she was supposed to squire around. She wanted to bolt to the street, but couldn't be that rude. The waitress came by. Daisy Cherensky bought them all a round of drinks. They talked over the music. Walter was a secretary in a state office.

"I work in a nursery," Cherensky said quickly, as if afraid Walter would talk for her again.

"I love babies," Inez shared. "Did you have to go to school for that?"

Cherensky screwed up her long-lashed blue eyes in a look of disgust. "Not babies. Trees, shrubs, birdbaths. That stuff."

"But that's heavy work," Inez protested. "I did it all through high school."

Cherensky shrugged off her jacket and stuck out a skinny little arm. She clenched her fist and said, "Feel that."

"The girl's got muscles on her toenails," confirmed Walter.

Inez laughed as she squeezed the bit of brawn. "I never would have guessed. How'd you get so strong?"

"Wheeling him around, for one."

"We've been best friends since high school," Walter explained. "She had to build herself up if she wanted to go anywhere with me." He leaned forward and whispered. "But I didn't know I was creating a monster!" Daisy Cherensky slugged him in the arm. "Ow! I'm ruined for life! Would you believe this one thinks she's butch? That's why I bring her down here, to learn to act like a lady."

Inez expected the woman to hit Walter again, but saw her go red instead.

"Drag her around the floor a few times, Inez, so she knows what she's missing."

"I'm not much of a dancer," Inez said. What good would it do to admit that she followed beautifully — they'd told her so back in gym class.

"I can ask for myself if I want to, Walter," Cherensky snapped.

There was another silence at the table. Inez wished some nice boy would approach Walter. He was so good-looking and funny, why would anyone mind his chair? Dancers packed the floor and the noise was raging.

"What?" she asked when she realized that Cherensky was talking to her.

"DO YOU WANT TO DANCE!" screamed Cherensky.

She tried not to stare in shock at this slight woman. Out of politeness she stopped herself from refusing.

"The Twist" was playing. Cherensky jostled a path for them onto the floor. Inez had learned the dance over at her parents' house from her brother's six-year-old kid. She did feel like a moose doing the twist above Cherensky, but the woman had a good sense of rhythm and didn't pay any attention to what Inez was doing. Inez caught Walter lifting his hands over his head in triumph like a champion athlete.

When the music ended, Inez grinned at Cherensky and turned to go to the table. Cherensky grabbed her hand and yanked her back. "Wait!" she shouted at Inez. "Maybe the next one'll be good too."

Inez waited, but when "Moon River" came on, she decided she'd just plain refuse to lead Daisy Cherensky around the floor. She shrugged. Cherensky boldly stepped up to her, put one hand behind her back and closed the other over Inez's hand. Was the woman nuts? Her head didn't even come to Inez's chin, for crying out loud. But before she knew it, they were out on the dance floor, close, and Cherensky was leading every bit as well as Kookie did.

Amazed, Inez closed her eyes. Cherensky's gentle pressures led her into the darkness where Inez filled to the brim of her full strong size. Inside, she bellowed along with the song. Under them, the floor seemed to rumble.

WHITTLING

"What do you think?" Jessie Malone said to the counterman in the coffee shop. "I moved out."

The counterman's mouth dropped open in his red, harried face. To Jessie's left, someone stirred coffee interminably. A toaster popped sickening fumes of food into the overheated air. Outside the steamy plate glass windows, a windless winter day froze the city in place. She took a deep breath and ordered a strong cup of black tea.

The counterman was still staring at her, not saying a word.

"Hey," Jessie said, trying for a joke, "life goes on, doesn't it? I have to fill my gullet with something, don't I, Morris?" Her hands shaped a flower from a napkin and she offered it to him.

"From Mary? You moved out from Mary?" Morris leaned across the counter and whispered, without taking the napkin. "And didn't I just make you that fantastic flower arrangement for your tenth anniversary? How *dare* you move out on Mary?"

With his hands on his hips, his too-black hairpiece and paunch, Morris looked to Jessie like a typical College Point fairy. He and his look-alike Jerome had been together almost twenty years.

"What do you mean, how *dare* I? She's the one who —" Her voice cracked and she thought she would choke. The words, when they came, were dry and unappetizing as burnt toast. "Who stepped out on *me.*"

"Nah," Morris said, dark brown eyebrows almost meeting his careful black wave. "*Mary?*"

"Shit!" stormed Jessie. Several heads rose from their plates and cups to take her in. She *wouldn't* cry.

Morris patted her forearm. "It's okay, Jess. Come on in the kitchen and cry on Mama's shoulder."

"No!" With a knuckle she roughly wiped one tear out from under her horned-rim glasses. "It may be okay for you to cry, but I'm no sissy." She rose and gathered up her two heavy suitcases, her shopping bag of woodworking tools and the string-tied shoe box which held the miniature carvings she'd planned to enter in the art show at the community center.

"Hey!" called Morris. "Where are you going? What

about breakfast? At least let me toast you a nice bagel!"

"I'm not hungry!" she yelled back over her shoulder.

With small, tight steps, Morris ran out from behind the counter. He wore his usual spit and polish black leather shoes and she stared down at them as she pushed her way backwards out the door.

"Jess! Let me help!" His shouted whisper barely carried over clinking cups, silverware and conversation.

She shoved one suitcase toward Morris with her foot. "Here," she said hurriedly. "Hold this for me, will you? I'll be back for it. I think."

"A suitcase? I want to fix your life and all you'll give me is a suitcase?"

"Let me alone!"

She walked as fast as she could along the slippery sidewalk with her remaining bundles until she turned the corner. Even the taxicabs crawled the streets with caution. Every little tree along the curb was encased in ice; trash was frozen to the gutter. She'd forgotten how desolate it could feel to be alone.

A dense gray sky promised no melting for today. She trudged on, muttering to herself. What did boys know, with all the fooling around they did? Her stomach growled. The shoe box, though lightest of her burdens, was the one which weighed most heavily on her mind.

She'd been preparing for the College Point Art Show for a year. Why did it have to be today? She'd gotten better since last year when she'd entered those big rough sculptures, balanced so carefully, and received an honorable mention. This year she'd been obsessed with learning careful detailing. It was the best feeling she'd ever had, working with those little pieces, using her delicate blades.

She wanted badly to spring her proud creations on the world, but Mary had organized the show. Mary, from whom she'd so carefully hidden her carvings, afraid of the criticism, afraid after Mary had taken college courses and become Arts Director at the community center, that she'd hate these primitive offerings. Jessie would have to face her in order to enter, would have to receive any prize from her. Would have to see the beloved face that no longer belonged to her.

One block up, she reached the jewelry store. She was too tired to stay angry, and so she stood at the curb across the street feeling forlorn. At least it was a Saturday and she didn't have to go in to the factory. It was no day to be a foreman; she'd be yelling at everyone. Probably get herself fired. See how Mary would like that, she thought.

Outside the jewelry store Hermine, a heavy bleached blonde in her forties, rolled back the grate with a clanking noise and cranked down the red-striped awning. Hermine went into the shop and returned with a bag of rock salt. Halfway through spreading it, she looked up.

"Jess!" she cried, stepping back.

Jessie crossed the street to her.

"Where have you been?" Hermine demanded, looking ominously oversized in her puffy red ski parka. "You scared the shit out of me, standing there making like a ghost. Don't you know Mary's looking all over the city for you? Where in hell did you go last night? You've got me and Beebo worried half to death."

Jessie put down the second suitcase, the shoe box and the shopping bag. "I was at the Y. Where else can I go when my girl finds somebody else three weeks after our anniversary? You can tell her to stop looking for me. I don't want to play second fiddle."

"You get yourself inside the shop, Jess. Beebo's in back. She'll give you some coffee. You look like you need it."

Jessie hesitated, but ten minutes later, in the back room, she was crying against Hermine's soft bosom. Her old friend's familiar flowery perfume mingled with the scent of silver polish. Beebo, nicknamed for a character in a gay novel, stood in the entryway, alert for customers. She was legally blind, and the stoop she'd had even in her sighted years had become more pronounced from peering at jewelry. She'd learned to do many of the routine repairs and Jessie would often find her leaning close to her workbench, feeling for imperfections.

"You *have* to work it out," Hermine said. "I don't care if she cheated on you. What chance does it give Beebo and me if you guys break up just before we get our ten years in? You think we're the perfect couple?"

"Why? What's wrong with you two?"

Hermine looked toward Beebo, who shrugged. "Just because she doesn't see too good," said Hermine, "doesn't mean this one hasn't got a roving eye."

"Beebo?"

"Lucky for her," Hermine went on, "I'm a very forgiving person."

"It was only the once," Beebo said, eyes downcast.

"In the beginning. I still couldn't believe you wanted me."

"So she has to go out and prove she's lovable, right? I told you, you should come to me, I'll show you how lovable you are."

"I have ever since, haven't I?"

"You have to tame them when they get a little wild, Jess."

"What do you want me to do?" Jessie sobbed into Hermine's sweater. "Climb into bed with them?" She sat up and shook her head. "All I want right now is to figure out two things. One, where I'm going to stay. Two, what I'm going to do about the art show." With her fingers she held onto the cushiony bulge of Hermine's waist.

"The show," said Hermine. "We finally get to see your work! I hear you wouldn't even let your girlfriend see it."

"My *ex*-girlfriend," insisted Jessie, trying to get used to the idea. It only made her start to cry again.

"So you say," retorted Hermine. "And what do you expect? You won't let her near your workroom where you spend half your life. What were you concocting in there, the atom bomb?" She glanced up at an ornate cuckoo clock. "It's ten now. When do you have to get your stuff there?"

"By noon."

Beebo, rangy, still leaned against the door frame, hands in her pockets, thick glasses slipped halfway down her nose.

"And they're doing awards when?" Hermine asked.

"Tomorrow at three."

"We'll be there," announced Hermine. "We want to see you get your first prize this time. Pam will know

168

good work when she sees it. Imagine, all the way from California to be one of the judges. Mary's doing a good job here, bringing College Point up in the world."

"Pam can get away easy. She's single," Jessie said.

"And Frenchy will be there with Mercedes. They've got almost eight years if you can believe it," added Hermine.

She felt so ashamed of her failure before all these friends. She and Mary had been the first in their crowd, the longest, the forever ones. Why her?

"If I could just die," Jessie said, slumping in her chair. "Mary's whole family will be there to see this show. For Pete's sake, guys, how am I going to make it without Mary's family? They've been better to me than my own. And I can't even tell them what Mary's done." She hugged her stomach, imagining that the pain would kill her off any minute. "I can't tell them about that stinking no-talent refugee from the midwest who's their next son-in-law."

Beebo shifted in the doorway. "I thought Verne was a painter."

"Yeah," Jessie said, balling up her handkerchief as if it was Verne. "If you like paint-by-numbers. She's a hustler. Paints five or six landscapes over and over and sells them at shopping malls. Her newest thing is selling everybody else's work. Says she wants to open a gallery and get rich."

Abruptly, she rose. Another wave of pain was approaching at the thought of Mary with such a conniving woman. Word was, Verne had moved into a lover's apartment, someone who'd gone to school in the midwest and dragged her back to College Point. Why had Verne gone to that workshop Mary organized? Why couldn't it have stopped there, not progressed to coffee after, dropping in at Mary's office, then a trip to a museum? Then — this.

Jessie wanted to outrun the pain. She thought briefly of drinking herself into a stupor as she might have in the past, but this time there'd be no brother-in-law Mario to rescue her. She'd never needed steadier hands or a clearer mind. She lifted her box of sculpture and her bag of tools. "Can I leave this suitcase here?"

"Where're you going?" Beebo asked.

She pushed the heavy suitcase under the work table, then bumped her way past Beebo. "I don't know. Away. The midwest maybe, where I can learn to be a skunk and hurt other people before they hurt me."

"What about the show?" called Hermine along the length of the sparkling counters.

Jessie shrugged, then struggled with the front door. A bus was slowing to a stop at the corner. She ran for it, the string around her carton cutting into the pads of her fingers. She would sit on the bus and think. But it pulled out in a belch of exhaust before she could reach it.

She turned toward the East River. Several blocks on was the garage where Del worked. That little grease monkey had the tightest thinking cap Jessie had ever run across, except for Mary. A lot of good Mary's would do her now. Jessie carried her pain to Del like one more heavy suitcase to be left behind.

Her fingers were numb from cold by the time she got to the garage. She saw Del working inside, a shadow in the oily-smelling building. Del didn't so much pass as a guy — she plain and simply looked like one, all the time, in every move and gesture. She was Jessie's size, a little taller than average, bulky but without curves, like a nicely blocked-out chunk of wood, thought Jessie. As always, she was head to toe grease.

Del wiped her fingers on a filthy rag and pumped Jessie's hand. "Long time no see, pal."

"Mary's been seeing somebody behind my back," blurted Jessie.

"I told you that dame would go dizzy on you," Del responded without a pause. She stuffed the rag in her back pocket. "Didn't I tell you that? You don't give her enough attention, barricading yourself in that workshop of yours or else staying at the plant overtime."

Jessie's hand felt like it had a sheen of grease over it. She had the urge to smell it, to be covered by grease or sawdust or whatever good earthy work would soothe her pain.

"I wanted to surprise her all at once! If she came in and saw what I was working on she might not like this one or that one. This way, I figured she'd at least like some of them." Jessie sat, carefully balancing herself on a stack of tires.

Del lit an unfiltered cigarette. "So you kept all of it from her, not to mention you kept all of you from her. So she went out looking for hands that wanted woman, not just wood."

Jessie came up in a crouch, fists squeezing tight on every ounce of rage inside her. "Fuck you!"

Eyes narrowed, cigarette between her lips, Del held Jessie at arm's length. "You come to me to get a pretty picture or what? You're the highfalutin artist. You go whittle yourself what you want to see. Me, I look at the insides of things, what makes them go."

Jessie stopped glaring. She rebalanced herself on the tires, the rubber threatening to collapse and spill her into the deep center hole. Del always made her mad; Jessie always ended up thanking her.

Del went on. "Mary's a good girl, don't get me wrong, but she's had it easy since she was a kid — first her old man at her beck and call, then you. She thinks she's been playing house with you all these years. What do you expect? You shut her out, she's going to find another playmate. She has no way of knowing yet that broken hearts hurt like hell and can't always get welded back into one piece."

She drew smoke in so long Jessie thought she'd see it come out of her shoes.

"So what do you want?" Del asked, finally exhaling. "You giving up for good, or you just trying to scare her, hauling your baggage all over heaven and earth like hearts on your sleeves?"

"I don't know yet. First, I have to find a place to stay. Second, I have to figure out by —" She looked at her Timex. "Noon, if I'm going to put my stuff in the art show Mary organized."

"I got the invite. Thought I'd go see if there's any photos of old Chevies this year. Remember that Kaiser picture I bought? I got it framed. That's my kind of art. You still doing those weird boxes?"

Jessie stroked her carton. "I've been trying little carvings. There's a couple cars in there I thought you'd like."

Del stomped on her cigarette until it was shredded. "Let's see."

172

"No." Jessie pulled the box to herself, fingering the rough hairy twine. "I might win something on them. There's only about four things that are real-looking like that. The rest are designs." Even as she said this, she knew herself to be lying. "That's not all of it, though," she confessed. "It's just habit now, but I guess I wanted Mary to see them first and when I was ready. It wasn't anything personal against Mary."

Del laughed. "And her side affair probably isn't anything personal against you either."

"That's different!" Jessie sputtered.

"Hey! She doesn't have wood to carve." Del craned her neck toward the office. "I have to get back to work. I'm not saying it was right, what Mary did, I'm just saying it doesn't have to be the end. Listen, I'll see you over at the community center."

"I might not go." She gripped her stomach again.

Del heaved a large sigh and once more glanced over at the office.

"What's the matter? You have a bellyache?"

"Yeah," replied Jessie, sweat forming on her forehead. "It's like I've got Mary inside me, carved down to a little nub that got stuck in my gut."

Del gave a short gruff laugh. "You whittled her down to size, huh?" She picked up some tools and motioned for Jessie to move to the car with her. "Look at this."

Jessie stared down into the depths of the car as if its guts were her own — rusted, leaking, complex. She closed her eyes against the pain.

"Me," said Del, "I learned not to get a dame mixed up with this vehicle's insides." She hitched up her pants and bent over to dismantle something. "Donna may be heaven for me, but this here is earth."

"So what would you do? If you were in this car-fixing contest, and Donna was giving the prizes, but she did what Mary did."

Del stood, blinked at her, then smirked and shook her head. She brushed herself off and set her tools by the side of the car, then lay flat on her back on a low dolly.

"You mean I'd have a choice? Hiding myself under a bushel basket or showing Donna my best damn work? She'd be lookin' at the very best of me?" Del wheeled herself under the car, laughing.

Jessie stepped to the open garage door. It was 11:30 now and icicles everywhere were dripping, then crashing to the sidewalks. The service bells sounded as cars pulled in and out of the station. A pump jockey leapt from island to island. The factories were quiet today, but the parking lot at the grocery across the street was packed, and a man with a hot dog cart was wheeling quickly toward College Point Park. She could smell the remains of Hermine's perfume on herself.

All her friends wanted her to stick it out. She'd had no heart for it earlier, for registering in the art show, for seeing Mary again. She'd never forgive her for doing it with that Verne person, but maybe it wasn't all Mary's fault. Maybe she had whittled away at their life together and ought to look inside to figure out why.

She called back to Del in the shop. "Can I leave my tools with you?"

"Right here by me, Jess. I'll put them in my car on my break."

A sharp wind came up from the river, but the sun quickly tempered it. The smell of toast stayed in its wake. Her mouth watered. She lifted her shoe box into her arms and cradled it. Was she going to throw all this away?

CACTUS LOVE
Windy Sands II

Until that night, I'd have bet my bottom dollar I
was a washout. It'd been ten years since I touched
my last woman in love. Too much like walking
barefoot onto a sprawling Prickly Pear cactus in the
dark. I just didn't have the energy for love.

Then Van came, with her youth and her brains. I
hired her to run the retail end of my cactus ranch.
That left me free to spend all my time on the
growing, the watering and — well, I ran out of things

to do. I'd watch that young body run around, enjoying the heck out of life. Even after her breakup with Ivy she was back in the saddle before you could say Jack Rabbit.

That was October. I can see her standing in the bright sunlight outside my trailer, one foot on the metal step, saying, *I'm going down to the bar tonight. Want to bet I find a lover before Christmas?* What'd she do then? Went out and got one. I confess that girl's been an inspiration to me. I went out and got one too.

Whoopee! I feel like dancing with my cactuses.

Billie is older than me by a couple of years, but she doesn't look like anybody's cute little grandma. Van called her the Matriarch, from the way the young ones at the bar would chew her ear.

I watched Billie.

I liked looking at her, sitting straight as a ruler's edge at the bar. She's part Irish, part Zuni Indian — tall, very skinny. Her bones are so broad and strong-looking you'd think she was some desert wild thing. Maybe that's what put me off at first. I'd always been one for your younger, femmier types. But Billie, she's not interested in all that. She's not butch, not femme. She's no garden-variety female at all. She's a monument. I could listen to her talk about her life all night . . .

But it wasn't listening I did that first night.

She had about as much stomach for that smoky, loud joint with its watered-down country jukebox as I did. She always left around 11:00, just before it got real loud and wild. I'd decided after the first few times I saw her that I wanted at least to talk to her. The next time I went to the bar, though, I dithered and dithered. Before I knew it, it's 11:00 and she's leaving and I can't think of a blamed thing to say to her anywhere as good as *would you like to dance?* I'd missed my chance. So I let it go another week.

But you know, she started coming into my head a lot that week. When I was in bed at night I'd imagine her, with that long, strong body next to me on the white sheets. I imagined the life story she'd tell. And I imagined her hands on me. I'd noticed them when I was next to her at the bar ordering drinks. Some arthritis, a little stiffness and knobbiness. Still, you got the feeling that bit of bother would be as likely to stop her as spines stop a wren from nesting in a cactus. I could feel the seasoned fingers on my hip, on the other parts of me that were never this cushiony for my earlier girlfriends. I kind of just ran her through my head, to see if I'd like it, or if I only wanted her because we were close in age. I'd get wiggly at the thought of Billie's touch. Not many women can seep into my head like she did, in the dark.

So the next Saturday night, that lulu of a night, I asked her to dance. She looked down at me and said nothing, nothing at all. But there was a little smile that puckered the corner of her mouth. And those brown eyes like polished jasper looked like they were laughing. Then she swept me out onto the dance floor. Swept me out there and danced me around those young couples like she'd put me on wheels. I never felt so light on my feet. That darned woman took my breath away. I never wanted the dance to end.

I asked her back to our table. Van was sweet-talking her new girl, so they didn't pay us much attention. Luckily it'd taken me till 10:30 to get up the nerve to buttonhole Billie. By this time it was getting on toward 11:00 and noisy in there. I told her about my business, asked her if she'd ever seen a cactus ranch by moonlight.

"Well, no," she said, laughing. "I can't say that I have, or heard such a barefaced line."

It turned out she lived near the bar and didn't have a vehicle. I drove her out here in Pickup Nellie, my old white Chevy. We parked behind one of the hothouses. Wonder of wonders, there was a moon shining down. Not quite full, but full enough. The moon looked like it was pounding up there in time to my heart. The night was pretty darned hot for November.

We walked out on the desert a ways, without a flashlight. She was wordless, quiet-moving. I was just enjoying the company, come what may. Big patches of waning yellow desert broom like earth-moons glowed at our feet. We didn't go too far so as not to disturb any critters.

On the way back, she took my hand. I thought I'd melt right there at her feet, like some little teenaged person.

"You want to come in?" I asked when we reached my trailer house.

"I didn't come all this way to turn around now," she replied, her teeth white against that sunburnt skin. There was a dogtooth missing. I thought of her moist tongue seeking out the empty spot, all alone inside her mouth. Holy Toledo, I know I'm a goner when ideas like that creep up on me.

Billie squints when she talks, like she's measuring you. "I've been noticing you at the bar," she said, over some iced coffee I threw together. "You're not my type at all."

I had to grin. "You're not mine either."

She nodded. "If there's one thing I have learned in my life, it's that you have to take things as they come. It doesn't do to fight your spirit, it always gets its way. If it wants to go changing my tastes in women at the ripe old age of sixty-nine, well then, I'm ready."

"Same here," I said. "I never wanted another girlfriend. All that heartache. But —" And I told her about Van's coming, and about the blood that got stirred up in my veins. "I could take the lonesomes," I told her, "till I started wanting again."

"I hear you. I sit in my little cement block apartment and tell myself I'll stay home with the cat, read a good book, watch the TV. I don't need that bar. It's not the liquor that calls me — half the time I order milk, trying to put some flesh on these bones." She lifted her arm like I could see the scrawniness under her striped jersey. "Maybe I feel useful there. The kids come and pour their little hearts out to me. Sometimes they think they want to get me into bed, but to tell the truth, their energy drives me up a wall. I'd never get any peace."

She paused, setting down her glass. "I'm thinking, little Windy Sands, maybe I could stand a change of pace."

I told you the lady was big. Those arms were long. She reached clear across my narrow tabletop. Now her eyes were like some wise desert creature's looking into mine for, I don't know what, for some kind of sign, I suppose. Then she kissed me, a little shaky from that distance, her hands kneading my shoulders.

181

And I kissed her back, giving her everything I had to let her know it wasn't just the kids who wanted her.

I stood. Led her to the bedroom, still with her hands on my shoulders, like she couldn't find her way without me.

"I guess we both know what comes next," I said, laughing. "But I'll keep the light out if you don't mind."

"Why, because you've got an old body?" she asked. "Hell, it's not even as old as mine!"

"Yeah, but you're slender as the needles on a pinion pine."

"I'm scrawny, you mean. And I have scars."

She switched the light on. I saw the scars. An artery taken out of her legs for heart trouble. Gut trouble where she'd been sliced open a couple of times. That took my mind off me. I was whole, even with this body round and pale as another earth-moon.

We lay full out against each other, like we were hungry. Like we were on fire and by pressing ourselves together we could put it out.

We held like that. We held like that for a long time. It felt so good, but it didn't put out my fire. The longer we held, the hotter I felt. I wondered if the same thing was happening to Billie, but knew I wouldn't find out till I reached between her legs, and it was too soon for that, old hands at this stuff or not.

After a while I started rubbing against her and rubbing against her, just the way we were, pressed together. She kissed me again, and I smelled the iced coffee and felt her sweat and the heat of our bodies in the trailer's hot air. Her skin felt slick, and marked like the moon. We kissed and pressed into each other. Then, swift as a crafty old rockdweller looking for shade, she wriggled her arm between us. Oh, she found out I was raring to go. I heard her exhale. I don't know for sure that she was excited before then, but hot-ziggety if that didn't do it for her.

She took her lips from mine and started kissing and licking my neck and my face, her tongue in my ear, in my mouth. I rode the heel of her hand like she was some fine horse taking me out across the desert under the blue blue Arizona sky, taking me up a mountainside, green and lush like it gets over on the east end of Tucson. We rode so fast I could hear the leaves stir from our passage until the sound of a rushing waterfall began to grow. She stopped so I could see, so I could feel, so I *was* that water falling from the mountain. Falling down and down and down and —

Tens years of bottled up pleasure. Everything spilled out of me.

What I said after that was, "I'm too darned exhausted to turn over. Can we talk for a while?"

"Sure thing, Windy, if you have the breath to talk. Was that too much for you?"

"Not enough," I panted, "not hardly enough, Billie."

It was the first time I heard that laugh of hers. The mysterious-sounding, low, back-of-the-throat laugh that reminds me of Frank Sinatra singing about "come hither looks" in my younger days.

She began then, telling me about the places she was raised in New Mexico. I tried to listen, but sleep came over me like a red-tailed hawk onto a tasty pocket gopher. All I recall is that it got too cold, nights up there in the mountains for her. She migrated south in her truck and got factory work where she could. Now she's retired.

I was out long enough for the moon to follow us to my bedroom, right inside the trailer window. Billie was asleep too.

Oh, the moonlight on that body. Billie was less than slender, she was as bony as an ancient saguaro turned brown and ribby. Hips, shoulders, rib cage — all made her like a cradle I just fit into. My hand waltzed over the juts and hollows of her. I felt weak — from exertion? Lust? Maybe all I needed was a little snack.

No, I couldn't leave the sight before me, the white moonlight on the deep-toned body. She was handsome as all get out.

It didn't take long until one of my caresses woke her. She opened her eyes and her mouth and groaned for me. I just plunged in then, wondering if she'd ever had babies, she was so big. Plunged one finger, then two, then a third. She made herself smaller around me. I was too short to reach up and kiss her. She was too hot to bend down to me. I rested my cheek on her breast, plunged harder, deeper, softer, slower, quicker. She brought her hands flat across my shoulders and drummed and drummed and drummed as she came.

"If I smoked," she said after a while, "I'd say that calls for a cigarette."

"Cigarette nothing, a ten-gun salute!"

We settled for my snack.

She sat up all grins, like a little kid going to a party. We padded to the kitchen bare-assed, dragged every darn thing out of that icebox we could find and had ourselves a feast.

Billie didn't stop beaming the whole meal.

What am I talking about? Looking at the gap in her teeth, the mussed gray hair, at those brown eyes like mirrors full of desert roads and pickup trucks, honkeytonk gay bars and jukebox-dancing women, full of sixty-nine years of love and disappointment and love again. Ah, geez, I knew I'd found somebody who was going to make all the mess and bother of love worthwhile, and I'm still grinning right back at her to this day.

A few of the publications of
THE NAIAD PRESS, INC.
P.O. Box 10543 • Tallahassee, Florida 32302
Phone (904) 539-5965
Toll-Free Order Number: 1-800-533-1973
Mail orders welcome. Please include 15% postage.

BODY GUARD by Claire McNab. 224 pp. A Carol Ashton Mystery. 6th in a series. ISBN 1-56280-073-6 $9.95

CACTUS LOVE by Lee Lynch. 192 pp. Stories by the beloved storyteller. ISBN 1-56280-071-X 9.95

SECOND GUESS by Rose Beecham. 216 pp. An Amanda Valentine Mystery. 2nd in a series. ISBN 1-56280-069-8 9.95

THE SURE THING by Melissa Hartman. 208 pp. L.A. earthquake romance. ISBN 1-56280-078-7 9.95

A RAGE OF MAIDENS by Lauren Wright Douglas. 240 pp. A Caitlin Reece Mystery. 6th in a series. ISBN 1-56280-068-X 9.95

TRIPLE EXPOSURE by Jackie Calhoun. 224 pp. Romantic drama involving many characters. ISBN 1-56280-067-1 9.95

UP, UP AND AWAY by Catherine Ennis. 192 pp. Delightful romance. ISBN 1-56280-065-5 9.95

PERSONAL ADS by Robbi Sommers. 176 pp. Sizzling short stories. ISBN 1-56280-059-0 9.95

FLASHPOINT by Katherine V. Forrest. 256 pp. Lesbian blockbuster! ISBN 1-56280-043-4 22.95

CROSSWORDS by Penny Sumner. 256 pp. 2nd Victoria Cross Mystery. ISBN 1-56280-064-7 9.95

SWEET CHERRY WINE by Carol Schmidt. 224 pp. A novel of suspense. ISBN 1-56280-063-9 9.95

CERTAIN SMILES by Dorothy Tell. 160 pp. Erotic short stories. ISBN 1-56280-066-3 9.95

These are just a few of the many Naiad Press titles — we are the oldest and largest lesbian/feminist publishing company in the world. Please request a complete catalog. We offer personal service; we encourage and welcome direct mail orders from individuals who have limited access to bookstores carrying our publications.